Reviews

Anne Marie Welsh, San Diego based Arts Critic and Novelist:

"Author Robert Gilberg is back on the road again with his second novel, *Twists of Fate*. Subtitled *A Folk-Rock Odyssey*, the new book continues Gilberg's love affair with the vast spaces of the American landscape and celebrates the iconoclastic spirit of poet-rocker, Bob Dylan. His late-in-life hero sets off on a journey to find a long-lost love and, like the car loving protagonist of Gilberg's Alice Chang, finds himself involved in a mystery and a thrilling climatic chase."

Jen Coburn, author of best seller, *We'll Always Have Paris:*

"A tale of love, loss and redemption that leaves readers wondering what they've left behind on the road not traveled in their own lives. With twists and surprises, this ballad of a novel rocks."

"Kirkus Reviews":

Gilberg (*Alice Chang*, 2016, etc) offers an offbeat romantic novel about roads not taken and second chances, underscored by a fondness for '60s music, specifically Bob Dylan's. . . .

The storytelling is solid, if mellow, and Gilberg doesn't make the mistake of reflecting on the '60s by checking off the usual laundry list of Vietnam, Woodstock, Altamont, Apollo 11, and so on. Nor does he overdo the Summer of Love nostalgia when all is disclosed about what happened to Dianne and her fellow Ohio refugees. A Dylan-infused novel that mostly pulls off its sentiment....

Twists of Fate

Twists of Fate

A Folk-Rock Odyssey

Robert Gilberg

ISBN: 099908870X
ISBN 13: 9780999088708

Contents

Prologue - 2010

Well, I'll be dammed, there comes your voice again . . .

—Joan Baez, "Diamonds and Rust"

E minor, E minor slid into an F sharp note, then back to E minor, all played finger picking style. So familiar, "Diamonds and Rust." The perfect song for my mood tonight.

Gentle late-night summertime Pacific waves quietly lap at the beach on the ocean side of the dunes that protect our little sea-side patio from the strong, Pacific storms of the winter months. Soft night time ocean breezes lightly rattle the shutters folded to the side of the open windows. The music flows from my computer's speakers—surrounding, caressing, and seducing me. It invites me to close my eyes and travel back two thousand miles and fifty years.

half a lifetime and a couple of light years ago

I'm stopped in my tracks and everything vanishes in waves of nostalgia as memories flood my mind. I'm time shifted out of this new millennium back to the '60s. I remember choices, decisions I'd made about my life and career—and a girl. But it's more than just that one song. YouTube is inviting me to play the entire *Diamonds and Rust* album, including "Fountain of Sorrow," "I Never Thought You'd Leave in Summer," the title song, and "Simple Twist of Fate"—songs written by Dylan, Baez, Jackson Browne—geniuses: my generation, my spokespeople, and my conscience. Reminders that I might have done things differently—and that I didn't.

The times in Joanie's song are the early '60s, when Baez and Dylan dominated the music scene in Greenwich Village. They were the nobility of the folk—about to become the folk-rock—world. Together they changed our music. He wrote remarkable music-poetry, and with her otherworldly voice, she sang it beautifully. Joanie captured that world, a moment frozen in amber, in "Diamonds and Rust."

Living then in Ohio, I wasn't an active participant of their world; my space was a galaxy away from the people creating that music.

But being a passionate observer, it was my world, too.

Now, on evenings like this when I've dropped the day's projects and hassles and want to let myself drift for a while, YouTube takes me into the music-time-space zone where I'd lived before—long ago. Zen moments that can become an hour—or hours, or stretch into the next day. Even days. In one of those Zen spells, I might reach for my dusty, fifty-year-old, Epiphone folk guitar. Eyes closed, my fingers still find them: G, D, C, D7, D minor, G7, C7, B minor, E, E minor, A, A minor . . . the open string chords at the far end of the guitar neck that gave wings to my generation's music.

"Diamonds and Rust" never fails to make me wonder, *what if I had made different choices fifty years ago . . . ?*

"Simple Twist of Fate" reminds me; *there are second chances . . . .*

Travelers - 1990

I spotted her sprawled on the sidewalk near the Greyhound bus station, just east of Highway 81. Her suitcase, a big blue boxy thing that had to weigh as much as she did with roller wheels and a telescoping handle was splashed wide open, teetering on the curb. The size of her suitcase said it all: *girl leaving someone, somewhere, somehow.*

On my Atlas road maps, Salina, Kansas, looked like it had to be just about the most dead-center small city in the entire USA. After spending the night in a La Quinta motel alongside a truck infested I-70 at the edge of Salina, I'd decided to see what I might find for breakfast in the most-dead-center-USA town, rather than eating motel food. Stuck at Bucks, a bar open for breakfast, had a few cars scattered around the parking lot. Either they were the cars of overnight bar flies who spent their night sleeping in chairs—or people who knew a good breakfast would be found there. It turned out to be both. The place smelled of stale beer and ashtrays full of cigar and cigarette butts with a few guys staring at themselves, comatose-like, in the big mirror behind the bar. But the eggs easy over with grits and bacon were the real thing: not the usual motel, gooey mess of Sterno-heated stuff in a warming pan with limp bacon cooked yesterday and cold breakfast potatoes probably left out overnight that even stray dogs had refused. I resisted the bartender's offer of a fish-bowl of draft suds for a buck and quietly ate my breakfast while reconsidering what the hell I was doing on this quest. But, looking around at the losers in the bar, I decided that having a dream that had me doing questionable things wasn't all that bad.

I paid the sleepy looking bartender and decided to see a little more of the most-dead-center-USA town before jumping the freeway and pointing the Jeep west. I wanted to get a feel for what it might be like, living hundreds of miles from anywhere.

It felt like Dayton, Ohio. Eleven and a half hours—772.6 miles and a day and a half on the road—and I was still in Dayton, except Salina is much smaller. Same looking single story business establishment buildings, bumpy streets and empty sidewalks, leafy trees and bushes, old homes on quiet streets, churches everywhere, train tracks with grain elevators, and muddy rivers and ponds. The clouds in the sky looked like Ohio's, and, according to my almanac, the weather wasn't much different.

It didn't feel like I was getting closer to California—more like I'd been running in place.

The drive had been boring: flat, monotonous, and dodging big trucks all the way. I imagined what it would have been like starting the drive where I-70 begins near Baltimore, Maryland. Probably more scenic back in the eastern parts with hills and low mountains, but not by much. And the truck traffic would surely have been worse. I-70, 1234.6 miles from Baltimore to Salina with endless truck traffic everywhere, nose to tail—like land trains— through the American heartlands. No thanks, I needed to get to the west coast, still well over a thousand miles away. Dylan's line from "One Too Many Mornings" kept playing around and around in my mind:

And I'm one too many mornings, an' a thousand miles behind.

On hands and knees, she was scrambling along the sidewalk and curb, trying to retrieve her escaping clothing, blowing away in the strong Kansas plains wind. Multiple mud puddles left by the overnight rains beckoned. A large, pink tote bag, still slung over her shoulder but dragging along the pavement, getting in the way, did not help her efforts. She wore a straw hat, like English ladies wear for gardening, that the winds kept blowing over her face. Dressed in a long-sleeved, man's white dress shirt over a pink tee shirt that matched her tote, and black jeans, she looked like a cover shot for *Life* magazine. Pretty, with her shirt tails hanging out over her jeans, wearing new-looking, matching pink sneakers, she was near tears. There was also a look of desperation. Pretty and desperate—and alone; the sight was heartbreaking.

I pulled over to the road side just past her and jumped out. "Let me help." I scrambled along with her, gathering up tee shirts and underwear, and held her by an arm to steady her as she slowly stood erect, wobbling a little.

"Oh, goddamn it! I'm sorry, I'm not cussing at you; I just missed my bus. But thank you!"

We shoved the things that had escaped back into the otherwise well-packed big blue suitcase, and I helped hold the top down as she forced the latches with ringless fingers.

"Where are you going?" I asked.

"San Diego."

"I'll take you over to the station and you can probably book another bus," I said.

"No, I looked up all the schedules and this is the only departure that would make the connections without a night in a motel."

"Can I take you to your home? Can't you just start all over again tomorrow?"

"It's not that easy; I'm leaving home. I left them a note telling them I'm going and don't know if I'll be back. If I do go back, I'll be stuck there forever."

"Do you mean your parents? Did you tell them where you are going?"

"Yes, I meant my mom and dad. I said I'd let them know when I got to my destination. I don't want them trying to anticipate it and have someone waiting for me there. I am over twenty-one, and can go where I want and do what I please."

"Look, I don't want to get involved in whatever is going on at home, but I'll help you if you ask. You look a little desperate to me and I'd feel guilty driving away leaving you in trouble. What can I do?"

"You aren't going west by any chance, are you?

"I'm going to California, too; so, yes, I'm heading that way."

Tears rolled down her flushed cheeks as she asked, "Will you help me catch up to the bus at its next stop, please?"

Wondering how bad things were at home for her to ask a complete stranger for a ride, I replied, "If I can, yes. But, are you sure you want to do that? I think I'm a pretty good guy, but you don't know me at all."

She looked directly into my eyes, "You have a wedding ring. Are you married and have kids? Do you have a daughter?"

Her innocent logic struck me and I thought about my own daughter: *How could a father walk away from a distressed young woman asking for help?* But I knew her questions had a different intent: *If you are a good father, you'd never abuse a young woman, would you?*

"Yes, I have two sons and a daughter. But you shouldn't take risks with someone you don't know from the man in the moon. You really should—"

"Then I think I can trust you. And I don't really have a choice," she said, tears flooding her eyes. Then, looking toward the nearby highway entrance, she asked, "If you don't want to give me a ride, I'll walk over to that highway entrance and hitchhike. I am going to leave here today."

I really didn't want to get caught up in something like this and was beginning to regret stopping to help with her suitcase and belongings. But hearing that word—hitchhike—I instinctively I knew I couldn't let her do it.

"Do you know where the bus stops next and when it departs?"

"Yes, I have the route schedule." She fumbled around in her purse and pulled out a folded sheet of paper with the Greyhound logo. "It's in Hayes, Kansas, and the bus should be leaving there at ten-thirty this morning."

"Okay, hop in. Let's go for it."

Her pretty smile shone through teary eyes. "Great! Thanks a lot. Can you help me with my suitcase? It's really heavy."

"Sure." I hit the Jeep's rear hatch release switch and lifted the monster into the Wagoneer's rear compartment.

"I'm Suze Arnold. That's S-U-Z-E, not S-U-S-I-E," she said as we fastened our seat belts.

And not S-U-E or S-U-S-A-N. I made a mental note to ask her later about S-U-Z-E, an interesting choice that caught my imagination. Suze said she was going to California to stay with an aunt and uncle who had visited Salina a year ago. They had been out touring the country in a giant RV and had stopped in Salina to visit Suze's parents. Aunt Julie and Uncle Mike had told her about living in San Diego and described the great beaches and other places to visit in the city. Suze didn't know Aunt Julie well, but she seemed like a fun person and had said they would welcome her if she ever wanted to visit them and stay awhile.

"Mom didn't think much of the idea, but I did. Uncle Mike liked it, too."

I pressed the Jeep over the speed limits whenever I could, but there seemed to be an army of highway patrol cars cruising I-70 or hiding behind overpasses. I didn't want to be stopped and ticketed, so I held my speed to a few mph over the posted speed limits. But the bus had a thirty-minute head start on us and had departed Hays for its next stop in Denver before we'd arrived. Not knowing the location of the Greyhound station in Denver made me realize her connection there could also be gone before we found it. I didn't want to spend hours wandering around, chasing and missing buses. I thought an alternative might be to drop her off at the bus station in Denver, whenever we got there, and let her work it out for herself. She could find a motel if necessary and rearrange her bus schedule and I'd be done with the affair. But the thought of my own daughter, Susan, being caught in a situation like that, fending for herself on the road, made me think of another alternative that seemed more helpful.

"Suze, I can drop you off at the bus station and you can take it from there, or you could ride with me all the way. I'm going to LA, so I could take you as far as you want to ride with me. It's up to you. I promise I don't have any hidden agendas."

"Would you? Well, I'd love it, but I can't afford motels; I was planning to sleep on the bus on the overnight parts. But if I could ride with you all the way, it sure would be much easier."

"Look, I've been planning on up-scale hotel-motels which cost three or more times as much as the kind you'd probably have in mind. But I'll compromise; we can find a Ramada or a Holiday Inn most places and I'll pay for both rooms and come out about the same. And, by-the-way, Suze, there are no strings attached. I don't want anything in return; just a good companion for the next fifteen hundred miles. It's a long boring drive, and having someone to talk to would be great."

I told her I had been considering going to San Diego, too. It had always seemed like the city I'd be most interested in if I moved to California. If she wanted, I'd take the extra few hours needed to drive her to San Diego before going back north to LA.

"I'm not on any schedule. Deal?"

Looking wonderingly at me, like you-gotta'-be-kidding-me, a little tentatively she said, "Well . . . sure. I think you are a nice person. Deal. But I am going to pay for my own rooms and meals."

"Okay, then. Here's my promise: anytime you feel uncomfortable with me, or anything, for any reason, just say so and I'll drop you wherever you want."

We pulled out of the Hays truck stop-bus station and back onto I-70, pointing the Jeep west, both of us California dreaming.

With three days and fifteen hundred miles in front of us, I wondered, *Great, now how do I bridge the generation gap with her? Will we be able to talk? Should I ask her about why she's leaving home?*

I figured the best thing to try would be to tell her a little about myself so hopefully she'd be comfortable doing the same. But before I found a starting point I hoped might get her interest, she said, "So, tell me about yourself."

Taken off guard, I stuttered and started, then restarted before finally diving into it.

"Well, I'm from Dayton, Ohio, and, as I mentioned, I'm headed for California. I'm looking for an old friend out there from back in the '60s. But I don't have a clue about where she is."

"She?"

"Aaaaahhhh, yes, she. But let me explain."

I told her the story of an old girlfriend named Dianne who'd stolen my heart but moved to California before our relationship had a chance to fully develop. And I told her of my marriage with Sara a year after Dianne left, and the family we'd raised. Suze didn't say a word but watched me intently the entire time, clearly taking in the entire story that had me talking for nearly an hour.

When I had finished, she said, "I'm sorry that you lost your wife. She sounds like she was a wonderful person. And it sounds like you have good children, too."

Then she asked, "But I'm curious about why you didn't go to California with Dianne. I mean, I heard you say you couldn't leave your new job just like that, but is that really it? It seems to me like if she meant that much to you, you should have gone. If it was me in that situation, I would have. I'm not saying you made the wrong choice, and it certainly turned out well for you, but a girl like that might only come along once in a lifetime."

Wow, she knew how to get right down to it without wasting any time. My only answer was a cop-out. "Suze, sometimes you just don't know what the right thing is at the big moment. I didn't, and I took the conservative way out. I let her go."

"Funny, to me the easy thing would have been to go with her. She was obviously someone you loved. I'd go with love."

Jesus Christ, she wasn't afraid to say what she thought to a total stranger about intimate topics. She'd opened me right up and would know everything about me before we got to Denver! But I didn't mind. I actually liked the idea of being completely open with this inquisitive, uninhibited girl, easily more than twenty years younger than me. Strange how it seemed easier to be more open with a stranger than with my own kids. It wasn't that I didn't have a good relationship with my children, but some things are just hard to talk about with them: like an old love . . . .

"What do you expect to find, if you do find Dianne?"

"Good question. I have no idea. Maybe someone who doesn't even remember me, or doesn't want to remember me? Maybe someone who does remember me, but wrote me off as a loser? Or maybe someone who will remember me and want to spend a couple of hours catching up, check her watch, tell me she's late for lunch and, 'thanks for looking me up' and we'll have to do it again sometime? I don't know, it's a little scary."

"Why do you care so much? What's making you do this?"

"It's hard to say. I guess it's just that I've thought about her now and then for over twenty years and have never been able to shake off the question of whatever happened to her. It's like a mystery I have to solve."

"Not a love you want to re-ignite?"

My God, she's peeling me open like an orange. "No, I don't think I'm ready for that, or even interested in that at this point in my life. I don't have any idea if I'd even be of interest to her."

"But you have no idea of what she's thinking, do you? Maybe it would be the perfect thing."

Over the past year, after the pain of Sara's death had subsided, I'd had that thought too, and it made me ashamed. But it always came back when the idea of doing the trip crept back into my head; maybe . . . .

But I always quashed it; *No way.* She's been out there in California somewhere, living a faster, more interesting life than my routine one in Ohio. She'll view me as a quaint, old hick-friend from Farmersburg, Ohio. And, of course, there's a high likely hood she's married. *Forget it!*

"Suze, I'll be happy just to find her, spend a day catching up, and leave as still good friends. That would make it a good trip."

"I hope it works out for you. I think you're a nice person; don't sell yourself short."

Where have I heard that before? And how does this young girl read me so well? It's like she knows me! I thought again about what had me making this trip . . . .

Dianne - 1967

Dayton, Ohio, is, by any measure, a long way from places like New York City and everywhere in California. But distance—mileage—is the least of those measures. They are places in parallel universes bridged occasionally by art that finds its way across the space and cultures that separate them.

With everything happening in the world of young adults in the '60s, primarily on the east and west coasts, what was I doing in Dayton?

The big cash register company planned to make a major push into mainframe computers and point of contact, on-line terminals. They wanted electronics and software engineers—or more accurately, lusted for them. I'd graduated in the spring of 1965 and they seemed like the right choice for me. A Fortune One Hundred company, a nice Midwestern city, not too far from—and not too close to—family. The money was right and the cost of living affordable. The easy choice.

But it was boring. After five years in Columbus with more than 30,000, twenty-something aged students, top sports teams, the party bars and great looking co-eds, Dayton was dead. Dead like they rolled up the streets downtown at seven pm and everybody went home. Dead like everyone living there grew up there; no one came from somewhere else. Dayton was not a destination city for adventuresome, educated young adults looking for an exciting start to their new after-graduation lives. Everyone there just kept on keeping-on with their high school and neighborhood friends and sweethearts. They didn't need to meet anyone new, including self-important elites moving into town with their shiny brand-new college degrees. Dayton was a blue-collar town with a middle-aged mindset.

Except for Dianne. Dianne who somehow decided to come home to Dayton as a new MFA graduate from OSU to teach at Antioch in nearby Yellow Springs. Why the hell she did that I never understood. She had offers to work in New York City and Washington, DC, and other offers to teach at some of the best liberal arts colleges around Ohio. And she couldn't explain it either, other than to say she was interested in Antioch's legacy of social progressiveness and students going into public service with a higher calling in mind. Being a part of that and sending hopeful twenty-somethings out into the world to create social change had been her goal. This was the sixties; we were going to change the world. We were going to desegregate the schools and businesses. We were going to end wars based on lies and expose lying politicians who told us it was a war that had to be fought: something about a Domino Theory . . . .

Or it might have been that Dianne wanted to continue her relationship with Mary, her apartment mate and best friend during their undergraduate years at Oberlin—and to teach at Antioch. It must have been both factors; I never understood it any other way. Mary was in love with Pete, an ace sports car mechanic who had a good thing going with his reputation as Dayton's best wrench. He wasn't about to leave his deal in Dayton, so Mary had returned home to him and taught in the Dayton school system. Dianne joined them in Dayton a year and a half later after finishing her MFA. It turned out that Dianne and I had been at OSU at the same time during our last years there, but we never met. Fine arts majors and engineering students rarely crossed paths.

Dianne enchanted me. She understood so much about things I knew little or nothing of: the arts, literature, social sciences, and world politics to name a few. An honors student at Oberlin, Ohio's top liberal arts college, with scholarships that rained down on her for her entire college life, Dianne was my oracle for everything in the political and art worlds. She'd graduated with a double major in political science and sociology before going on for her MFA in creative writing at OSU. Politics and political theory, socialism and capitalism, and the masters of the literary world were her intellectual backyard. I was an engineer who dealt with electrons, physics, math, and computer programming languages.

"Please, don't try to explain the difference between Fortran and Cobol to me, and I won't try to tell you why I like Pynchon more than Capote. If you do read them though, we could talk about it. But I'm not going to learn Fortran so we can discuss computers. Do you want to talk about music?"

Common ground! As a frequent guest on the Carson late-night show, I knew about Capote. But Pynchon? Never heard of him; probably because as a contemporary of Kerouac whose *On the Road* made no sense to me and didn't inspire me to wander around the country, I wasn't reading the beat writers. And Kerouac's laziness in the structure of his scroll version offended me: *Please, let's have a paragraph here or there, or maybe a chapter title now and then?* How could an engineer who had to write convincing technical papers relate to that?

But we could talk music.

She even understood what Dylan's songs meant. At least she gave convincing arguments for why they meant what she said they meant. I had my own ideas about them, but hers sounded better. Sometimes I faked knowing what she meant when she used references she would pull up at a moment's notice to justify her arguments. She was usually at the center of conversations about Dylan when there was a group of us listening and talking about his music. I was usually at the periphery of those debates, having little other than my own poorly informed thoughts. After all, I struggled to read and understand poetry and was clearly at a decided disadvantage to the rest. Most tech geeks had next-to-no knowledge of the obscure concepts Dylan used in his music, but at least I could dig some of his more obvious phrases—assuming I actually did understand them—and his melodies all felt natural to me.

Funny how being able to quote someone, or pull up a reference once read in a book written by someone I'd never heard of would be so convincing. Dianne did it at the snap of a finger—like Dylan. And even if I didn't understand all of it, I believed in her enough to accept what she said. She was very understanding about my limited ability to decode Dylan, and patient, non-patronizing care—and a joint or two—helped me through it. She could convince me of anything; I wanted to be convinced. A line, from "Queen Jane

Approximately, *"Now when all the clowns that you have commissioned, have died in battle or in vain . . ."* had mystified me for months.

"It just means he was telling Baez that he wasn't going to be one of her foot soldiers in the battles for social reforms—going to marches and demonstrations and all that. It was around the time they started going their separate ways."

That surprised me; I thought he was the general leading the charge. I accepted it but didn't know enough about their personal relationship to fully understand it. But who could know, anyway? He seemed to constantly be contradicting himself. It had sounded a lot more mysterious and exotic to me, so I was a little disappointed to find that's all the line meant. But I found the melody and rhythm grooves in that song captivating enough to love it anyway. Strangely, the more obscure the words and lines, the better I liked the song. Too often, once I understood that many song meanings were pretty ordinary, I began to lose interest. The less I understood them the more I liked them, and the more I wanted to listen—trying to figure them out. But, they had to rock!

Dylan's best lines stuck with me and I would add them to my lexicon for future use. I figured I was very cool quoting Dylan's lines when I could inject one into a conversation where I believed it fit the topic. But I had to be very careful doing it with Dianne in hearing distance. If I misused one, she'd be sure to correct me later in her friendly, teasing way. She'd told me the vagueness of his lyrics allowed a great deal of freedom in interpretation, to the risk of the interpreter—and woe to those who really missed the mark—so be careful around would-be Dylanologists. But there weren't many of those in Dayton, Ohio.

Dianne was a great companion for sitting around my or her apartment, listening to and debating the era's newest music. She was very pretty—and usually the one who managed to come up with a joint to smoke when talking about the world and listening to Dylan's latest. Smoking a joint was the best way to listen to him—it freed the mind—just as, I'm sure, he would have wanted. I assumed that he wrote most of his music in a fog, so listening in a fog seemed to be reasonable reciprocity. Like all engineers, I liked symmetry.

She was the ultimate cool, well ahead of most of the girls in Dayton in the sixties, with her wardrobe of black leotards or fishnet stockings, miniskirts, lipstick but no other makeup, pumps or heels—never sneakers—and her long, straight chestnut hair. She was completely open to almost anything, and passionate about Dylan's music. But she'd also listen to jazz and classical. She hated "bubble gum rock" like the Four Seasons, the Beach Boys, Neil Sedaka, Fabian and the others of that genre.

She dated a few guys, none of them steadily, but occasionally was out of touch on weekends. She never talked about those disappearances, and I was hesitant to ask. I just accepted them as another of her mysteries—another intriguing thing about Dianne. Most Ohio girls were open books; what you saw was what you got. Not Dianne.

Initially, she didn't want to date me in the usual sense of the word, but she wanted to hang out with me; I was to be her friend. But I did get to kiss her now and then. A hint of the possibilities . . . .

We'd have long, involved conversations in a little, dark bar that aspired to be a night club in south Dayton. It was in a residential neighborhood, surrounded by the homes of people who wanted nothing more than a quaint neighborhood bar. It was neither, which differentiated it from too-common strip mall bars or upscale, overpriced downtown clubs. It was a good place for those conversations: private, quiet, and friendly. And a sports car club met there weekly for beers and to talk about the problems they were having getting parts for their MGs and Healys, and Alfa Romeos. Which is how and where I met her.

My brake pedal had collapsed to the floor and brake fluid pooled under the car in my apartment's garage. The landlord was after me to fix it and clean up the damn mess. I'd been told about the Lamplighter by a guy at work who knew several of the sports car people who met there on Thursdays. I took his advice and went there the following Thursday evening to meet them and a guy named Pete.

Pete sat at the end of a long table full of people, with a girl on his left and one on his right. Both seemed to be with him. He was the main attraction—the one everyone deferred to in their conversations about the best crankcase oil or brake fluid to use in their cars. He enjoyed himself immensely—the center of conversation answering questions and giving out advice or telling about a new experience he'd had working on a new Jaguar coupe or other hot sports car. I asked if I might join them at their table and Pete answered first with, "Sure man, have a seat. Tell us about what wheels you're driving!"

"I'm Tom Paterson and I'm driving a 1961 Alfa Romeo Giulietta roadster—with a leaking master cylinder."

"What? Man, are you driving it that way?" Pete asked.

Nodding, I said, "I don't have any choice until I can find a replacement. I keep topping it off with more fluid, which I realize is a bad thing to do. It keeps getting worse."

Pete pulled a little notebook from his shirt pocket, flipped to a certain page, and gave me the name, phone number and address of a place up by Cleveland to contact for ordering a new master cylinder, telling me that they're great people who understood the difficulty in getting parts for Alfas. They'd put it on a Greyhound and have it to me the next day if I sent them a money order first.

After that piece of advice, Pete introduced me to the entire group sitting at the table. Mary, on Pete's right, was the first person I was introduced to, and Dianne, sitting on Pete's left, was the last person I met.

"Hello, Tom, I'm Dianne Wolfe. Nice meeting you," she said, looking directly at me with bright, sparkling grey eyes, slightly squinting because of her huge, broad smile.

She seemed so open and friendly that all my instincts were telling me to reach out and take her hand, but I really wanted to hug her. Smiling my best smile, I had to settle for, "Hi Dianne." And I followed that by the only thing I could quickly think of: "Are you driving one of those cool MGs or Porsches out there?"

She took my stupid question in stride, "No, I drive a big banana yellow Buick that I wouldn't be caught dead parking here."

She moved her chair to the side, inviting me to grab a chair from the next table and squeeze in between her and Pete. She explained that she had ridden there with Pete and Mary and that she always bummed rides with them to these "sporty car people" get-togethers. Her own car, the well-used, lumbering Buick Le Sabre, had been given to her as a graduation gift by her father.

I was a little amazed by this, knowing the tiny space in an Alfa Romeo coupe's rear luggage area. She had to sit sideways back there on the luggage shelf that might double as a child's seat. It was okay for a few miles, but anything longer was torture. It impressed me she did that just to be with friends for an evening. She didn't seem to be hung up over any inflated sense of dignity or femininity that would get in her way.

Later, when Dianne and I had a chance to talk, she told me that Pete and Mary were considering marrying sometime in the future—possibly as soon as the next spring time. But they weren't engaged, so it apparently was more of a mutual understanding that it would happen—someday. Dianne had been Mary's best friend in high school and through their undergraduate years at Oberlin. When she returned to Dayton, Mary, Pete, and Dianne became a threesome, nearly always together, at movies, clubbing, and even shopping. After I got to know her better and had cautiously asked about their closeness, she explained, "Silly, it's not a ménage de trois, we're just really good friends."

But Dianne and Mary did have a hands-holding, embracing and even an occasional kissing relationship—bold for the times, and very out-of-place in Dayton. Their affection for one another was mostly a closet affair that I hadn't noticed at first, but in off moments when they were away from the main group, it became more evident. I did think it curious that a girl like Dianne, who dated a number of other men in Dayton during our early friendship, had such an intimate relationship with Mary. But I never asked about it.

Mary and Pete lived together in an apartment in south Dayton not far from Dianne's. They were clearly in love. Dianne and Mary's relationship, whatever it was, didn't seem to be in the way.

I'd never known a girl as forward and open in meeting someone new as Dianne. In no time, she'd discovered my interests in music and literature, my political and social views, and what I did with my spare time. We'd spent another two hours after the Alfa Romeo master cylinder discussion talking together over icy Manhattans. We laughed when she said she'd had enough beer at Oberlin to last her the rest of her life. She laughed easily. I agreed with her about the beer; I felt the same way. We talked about how sad faced LBJ, being full of too much ego and 'Merican Power steroids, had taken us farther into the Vietnam mess and now was in too deep—how no one believed anything McNamara and Westmoreland had to say anymore, and how unbelievable it was that the Republican Party had tried to push Goldwater on us as a reasonable presidential candidate in the '64 election. And of course, we talked about the civil rights campaigns of the day. All of which brought us to music: Dylan, The Beatles, the Stones, and other social protest music of the day. Or any music that just plain rocked us. I wanted to dance with her.

As the group started leaving, I was wondering how to ask about staying in touch when she said, "I've really enjoyed meeting you and talking tonight. I'd be happy to have you as a new friend. I hope we'll be seeing each other more."

"Me too, Dianne! Can I call—" Thinking, *Oh, Yeah,* when she cut me off saying, "But I'm not putting the make on you. I don't mean it that way. You and I have a lot in common when it comes to music and politics, and it's fun to have a conversation with you. I was just hoping we'd get together occasionally: do a movie, take a drive, or come to these Thursday get togethers. No pressures, no implied responsibilities . . . just friends, if you know what I mean?"

I was surprised she had been so quick pointing out that she meant it to be a casual friendship. But nothing more? I didn't want to be intrusive by asking for clarification, so I let it pass.

"Aaaaahhhh, yes . . . sure! I'd like that too!"

Believing she wouldn't have said it without good reason, and not wanting to make her uncomfortable explaining herself, I decided the offer of friendship was good enough. A little disappointing, but not that disappointing; who knows where it might eventually lead? And, having a bright, easy-to-talk-to, pretty girl as a new friend couldn't be all that bad. I figured that time was on my side: Mick Jagger and the Stones were telling me so . . . .

Could I dig it? Hell yes!

⁓

"Do you want to go to the sports car races at Put-In-Bay next month?"

Dianne asked me that several months after we'd first met. By then we'd spent many evenings together—on her terms, so the relationship was still mostly just as friends. We were at the Lamplighter, sitting at the long table with a dozen others who were all making plans for the trip up to Lake Erie's South Bass Island a few miles off shore from Port Clinton. The Sports Car Club of America was proposing to renew racing for small bore sports cars on Put-In-Bay's upgraded old street circuit. Put-In-Bay had been a favorite of the Midwestern sports car racing crowd in the '50s, but accidents happened that gave it a reputation as too dangerous. So the racing—and the famous partying—had ended. Now there were plans to eliminate the hazards and restore racing on the famous island.

"Sure, what's the date? Who's going," I asked.

"Everyone here, including me if you'll go and I can ride with you. Come on, Pete's going to be driving his Porsche in the races. We have to go watch and cheer for him!"

If I can ride with you? Are you kidding me? "Yeah, sure, I'll drive. I'd love to go up there with you! What are the arrangements? Is someone booking motel rooms?"

"Motel rooms! No, this will be sleeping bags in the city park, silly," she said.

"Oh, well that sounds like fun. A big sleep in—or sleep out! What if it rains?"

"We're taking tents," several people said at the same time.

That sounds like even more fun, I thought to myself, visualizing the prospect of cozying up with Dianne in my pup-tent. *Maybe I should hope for rain?*

"I have a tent we can share if you don't have one," I offered.

She just smiled at me. Did that mean, *"Of course"* or *"Don't be silly"*?

A week later, at our usual meeting in the Lamplighter, we found out that the races had been canceled because the organizers hadn't been able to bring the circuit into compliance with insurance regulations. With a weekend suddenly available and a girl who seemed to be open to almost anything, I proposed to Dianne that we go for a day of racing at a famous old oval short-track racecourse in Indiana.

"It's around two hundred miles from here, so it's a full weekend. We drive over on Saturday, find a motel for Saturday night, and watch the races on Sunday. They should end around four pm and then we'll head back to Ohio. We should be back here around midnight, Sunday. Are you okay with that?" I asked her.

"I'd love to go! As long as we get back so I can get a few hours of sleep and over to Yellow Springs by nine Monday morning, I'm okay with it."

"Great!"

"But since you live on the east side of town and are at least thirty minutes closer to Antioch, I might want to spend Sunday night at your place. Would that be okay?"

Would that be okay? "Sure, you can leave your car at my place Saturday morning."

"I have an even better idea. Why don't I stay at your place Friday night so we can leave as early as we want Saturday morning? No extra driving that way. I can come over after my last class Friday afternoon and I'll avoid the hassle of driving across town in Friday evening traffic. I can pack my things Friday morning so we won't have to stop at my place. And we could fix something for dinner at your place, if you'd like," she said with an inviting smile.

This keeps getting better and better! "Great idea, I'll give you a key and you can let yourself in. I'll pick up some steaks and wine on my way after work. She gave me an excited little kiss on my cheek, saying, "And I'll make a salad and start baking some potatoes. Six o'clock okay?"

Yes. Hell yes! I had a one-bedroom apartment with one double bed: no foldout guest bed in the living room. The couch was comfortable for a nap but not overnight sleeping.

"Dianne, I don't have much to offer in the way of sleeping accommodations. It's just a one bedroom apartment and . . . ."

"I don't need much. You probably have a double bed, don't you? Just give me half of your bed and blanket, and a pillow. You stay on your half, and I'll stay on mine," she merrily said, as though it was nothing unusual. "It's not a big deal, is it?" That revelation, whatever it meant, amazed me more than a little. It was a big deal—for me!

I was falling in love, even if she only wanted me as a casual friend. And I was fascinated with the prospect of sleeping next to her—even if I wasn't going to be able touch her. I'd be able to smell her hair, her perfume—her essence . . . .

Or even more might happen, who knows? Thinking about it made my heart pound.

Lay Lady, Lay . . . .

Our fun Indiana weekend only made me fall more in love with my platonic friend. I struggled to go along with her rules on bed sharing at my place on Friday night and in our Indiana motel that Saturday night. But at least there, in the motel room, she'd slept with her back against mine, cozily pushed tightly against me. During the night, I thought I'd take a chance, and as I turned over to place my arm around her waist, she murmured softly that it felt nice, but to stop there. *Still, it was a step forward . . . .*

Driving back, approaching the Indiana-Ohio state line, she said, "Pete, Mary, and I are planning on going to California. Would you like to come with us?"

"A vacation? When and for how long? I'll have earned a week of vacation I could use in late August. Does that fit?"

"Tom, it's not a vacation. We're not coming back; we're going to move there. We're planning on leaving this fall."

What? My heart sank with the prospect of losing this girl I was just getting to know.

"Oh God, Dianne; just like that? You're leaving and moving to California? Why?"

"I made a mistake coming back to my hometown. Especially this town. There's nothing here I want anymore. It's boring, Midwestern, and, except for you, I'm not meeting anyone who's interested in my interests. I want you to come along."

"Oh man, Dianne; I just got a great new assignment and finally have settled in my new apartment. How do I pick up and move already? Why couldn't I have met you and had this conversation long ago—before I accepted my job? I'd love to go, but I don't see how . . . ."

"You can do anything you want, Tom! You don't have that much responsibility at your company yet. You're not married with kids in school and clinging grandparents—and you don't owe anybody anything. Come on!"

"I don't know . . . ."

"You should; you're your own person. There's nothing happening in Ohio. It's all either in California or New York. The music, the arts, even the jobs! Look at what's happening in San Jose and LA: all the new technologies and new companies. Don't sell yourself short; you'll be right at home there. Please don't be a drag and miss out on this. I want you with us . . . with me."

What could I say? Quitting after just taking a new assignment and a little over one year with a company was a black mark on anyone's resume. But was I turning her down over a job? And the last thing I wanted to think of at that moment, but churning around in the back of my mind was the conversation I'd had with my mother when I told her I had accepted the job in Dayton. But I did think of it: "Tommy, that's wonderful! I was afraid you were going to go to a city somewhere far off and we'd never see you. Now you can come home for dinner on Sunday, or even for a weekend now and then. I've been afraid you'd go to Florida or California, or some other racy place."

Racy meant loose morals, divorces, adultery, drugs, sex and skimpy swimming suits—the stuff she read about in the *STAR* weekly. And how would I explain running off to California with a girl I wasn't married to?

It wasn't that I would be afraid of disappointing my mother; I'd done that far more than once already. It was that I didn't want to go back over that decision again. I'd made it and wanted to stick with it.

"I told you I want you to be my casual friend, but not a romantic friend, remember?"

"Yes, sure I remember that. I didn't know what you really meant, though."

"The reason I told you that is during our first conversation I realized I could really like you. I mean, like maybe even love you. But I don't want to fall in love with a man who I'd probably end up married to and being stuck in Dayton. Or any of these Midwestern towns, for that matter. It just wouldn't work for me: raising a bunch of kids for the rest of my life. I'd be driving you crazy after not too long, and it would turn in to a bad scene that I would never want to happen to us."

"I don't think you're giving me a chance. How do you know I want to spend the rest of my life there?"

"I can't explain it. I guess it's instinct, or maybe the fact that you chose to live in Dayton in the first place when you could have gone anywhere."

"Well, what about you? You could have gone anywhere too. Why are you in Dayton?"

"Mary, Antioch, my dad . . . not so different from you. But I realize now it was the wrong thing for me. And I've realized I don't want to teach; I want to do something with my MFA in a writing field. With Pete and Mary going, it seems like the right time—before it's too late to make changes."

"Why does Pete want to go? I thought he loved his work here?"

"He's realized the west coast is where everything is happening in high performance sports cars and racing. He's fascinated with someone out there named Carol Shelby and his Cobra cars."

"But why not give me some time? Why does it have to be right now? Give me some time to work this out. I don't want to go out there, hat in hand without a job, looking for a job. That's a weak position that makes my background look questionable. I need to send out resumes and have interviews while I'm still working. That's when you have the best bargaining power."

"If you are a good prospect that really doesn't make any difference. I'm afraid you won't push it hard and just settle for things as they are here, and that you'll be trying to convince me to stay. Look, Tom, I've been hoping that going on this weekend trip with you would help you make this decision. I can't do any more."

Oh, my God. How good—and sad—it sounded hearing her saying that. After too many frustrating years in college, failing miserably in attracting the interest of any of the thousands of girls on campus, here was one pleading with me to go to California with her!

And now I'm going to turn her down and lose her?

I've thought a million times since then about how, in spite of her rule about each of us staying on our own sides of the bed, when I touched her shoulder that last night together back at my apartment, she turned over and reached for me. We pulled ourselves into each other's arms, head to toe . . . . There was no more holding back.

In the following days, I equivocated, procrastinated, worried and analyzed to death the idea of moving with her. It should have been easy. She was right; except for a car loan, I didn't owe anyone anything. I'd paid all my college expenses myself through part-time and summer jobs. And I'd made no promises to anyone, including my family. My decisions were my own, with no pressure from anyone. I was free—or I should have been free.

"If I come out in another year, or as soon as I get a new job lined up?" But that sounded stupid as I said it. What made me think she'd still be there, waiting for me?

"You could do that, Tom. But I can't make any promises. Who knows what could happen: you might change your mind, I might find someone, you might find someone, the world could end . . . ."

"If I drop everything and come out now, what happens with us? Do we get married? Or do we do as Pete and Mary; just live together?"

"I don't know. I don't want to make your coming along contingent on us getting married. I'd like it to go on just as we are now and let things take their natural course. I like us this way."

What was *this way*? Platonic friends who'd had *a moment*? It was the vagueness of it all that made me hesitate and eventually stopped me. None of the three had any concrete plans set for after their arrival in California. They weren't even sure where in California they were going: LA, or San Francisco, or possibly San Diego?

Not sure about where? And they didn't have any connections anywhere out there: no family, close friends, or even old friends. The plan seemed to be to cruise out there, city to-be-determined—but probably LA—arrive and drop anchor. Granted they were clever, ambitious people—but just drive out there, set up in some cheap motel and see what they could make happen? I was too much of an engineer for that. I had to have a plan. I had to have known facts, options, and back-up scenarios.

And what if Dianne and I fell out from each other?

I couldn't do it. How could I allow myself to get into a situation where I'd possibly be walking away from all those efforts and investments I'd made in my college degree in exchange for an unknown outcome, even if it was with this attractive girl? Ironically, the first girl in my life who'd shown serious interest in me but who might find someone else? I didn't consider myself to be a great physical prize, and the male competition in California would have to be intense: Hollywood, Malibu, Santa Monica, Newport Beach? Hollywood-good-looking, surfer-blonde, wealthy, California guys? My low self-confidence with girls needed more certainty than I was being offered. I didn't think I could compete in that imagined world.

And we'd never said the words "I love you" to each other.

Finally, a few days later, I said, "Dianne, you don't know how hard this is for me. I think I've been, or maybe I even already have fallen in love with you, but—"

She cut me off. "I'm sorry about this; I knew what your answer would be days ago. I really want to have you with us. We're good together, but I must do this, so don't try to talk me out of it. I'm not staying here."

We went back to being just the good friends we'd been before the California issue came up: good but platonic friends. And the elephant in the room was always there. The final weeks were miserable for me.

We still hugged and kissed occasionally when we got together, which happened less and less as the final weeks passed. But it was rigid and devoid of any passion. We were both holding back from each other, and our relationship was spiraling down. We'd given up. And we never again shared a bed after that weekend of the Indiana trip.

I had gone to see her at Pete and Mary's apartment for the goodbye party they held the night before they left. It was awkward and sad. We had nothing meaningful to say to each other, and she seemed to be avoiding looking directly into my eyes.

"Well, I guess this is it. I'm going to miss you, Dianne. Good luck." Cardboard words, meaningless . . . .

"I'll call, I promise. I'm going to tell you all about how much fun we're having to make you jealous." Throw-away words, also meaningless.

We did kiss and hug goodbye as I was leaving, but it was more like we did it because we should do it, rather than because there was love in it. I left her in the room where they were packing going-away mementos and talking excitedly about the trip. As I went through the door, she gave me a short, sad glance with a frozen half smile, and a quick little finger-wiggle wave. It didn't seem enough, but nothing was going to be enough. I couldn't blame her if she'd moved on.

They left in September, 1967, and despite her promises to keep in touch, I never heard from her after that night. Dylan's music haunted me: *Don't Think Twice, It's All Right* . . . . Only twice? More like infinitely . . . .

Others in the Lamplighter group did hear from them. Pete called one of the guys, Bob, a couple of times to let him know they were in LA, and he was checking out jobs as a mechanic at various sports car dealerships around the Hollywood area. The pay was fantastic compared to the shops in Dayton. The upscale dealerships that sold Jaguars and Mercedes and Ferraris to the glitterati in Hollywood and Santa Monica had plenty of money to pay top wages. In a later call, he said he was working at a new Porsche dealership in Santa Monica. He would get to help prepare the dealership's and customers' race cars for upcoming races and accompany the teams. He was excited to learn the racing game from inside well-funded teams with top drivers.

Mary called one of the Lamplighter group girls, Emily, a few times in that first year to tell them she was doing well. She'd found a terrific position in a big real estate development firm that was on fire building expensive custom homes in the Beverly Hills and Newport Beach areas. Surprisingly, in the first call, she said Dianne had dropped off the trip to stay for a while with a favorite aunt and uncle in Kansas before coming on to join them later in California. She said she believed it would be easier for just Pete and Mary to get jobs and a living place without her along. It seemed strange to everyone since Dianne had been such a staunch advocate of the move.

Many months later, in another call, Mary said Dianne had finally rejoined them and had taken a position as an intern reporter with the *LA Times*, working the city political beat. Her work as an editor of the *Oberlin Review* and as a reporter with the *Ohio State Lantern*, together with her MFA in creative writing gave her the background needed by the prestigious *Times*. Dianne had taken a cute little single-bedroom apartment on the same floor, in the same apartment building as Mary and Pete's. The three were still close companions, spending time together and seeing the sights in LA. Dianne dated only occasionally, but she didn't seem interested in any of the men after the first or second date. Just playing the field, Mary guessed.

I was getting the information from the Lamplighter group weeks after they got it from the three. Or—the two; Dianne never made any of those calls. And she never sat in on any of them by joining in from a second telephone. She seemed to be intentionally staying out of touch, letting Mary handle the conversations. But Mary and Pete always swore she was happy and well. She loved her job and worked it seven days a week. She seldom ate meals with them any longer, though; usually picking up carryout to eat at her desk while she worked on a hot story.

With Pete, the driving force behind the group gone, the Lamplighter people rarely got together again. I saw them even less and gradually lost contact with the group—and my second-hand updates on Dianne.

I was happy for all three, after having imagined the worst: one, or even all three, ending up as drug addicts, or being taken advantage of by a slick hustler who would take them for the limited amount of cash they had. Or Mary, or Dianne, or both, ending up dancing on runways, dollar bills stuffed into G-strings to stay alive as so many star-struck, beautiful girls reportedly did after hitting the wall trying to make it in poor-paying straight jobs out there. Or maybe they'd end up in a ditch: raped, robbed, murdered, and discarded. Nothing was too far out for my Midwestern imagination and concern after reading about the Manson murders later in '69.

I'd been thinking just like my mother—that the worst case was always what would happen! But I believed—or hoped—those three were too good to end up like that. I hated myself for selling them short. I hated myself even more for selling myself short.

Living in Dayton, I felt I was missing everything going on at the time: being there where things were happening in music concerts, love-ins, protests, and free spirited young people asserting themselves. And I could only listen to it happening on the radio, or on the latest Baez or Dylan LP album, or watching it on TV. I was a long-distance spectator, watching life in the sixties as it happened—through binoculars. But, like looking through binoculars from the wrong end, everything was far, far away . . . .

And I missed her: *honey I want you, I want you, I want you, so bad* . . . .

But, by my own decision, I had lost her.

Rescue - 1968

I tried to bury myself in my job. My sort-of-okay, average, well-paid, I-can-live-with-it job. But my heart wasn't in it and it showed. My work was uninspired, my reviews and salary increases were mediocre, and I second-guessed myself over Dianne daily. Even the music I loved began to depress me because I realized the people making that music were moving around: going to California, New York, England, or around Europe, having the times of their lives. The winter of '67 came to Ohio and the music on the radio made my decisions, nailing me into small city Ohio, seem all the worse. "If you're going to San Francisco," "California Dreaming," and "California Girls" all made me more miserable. I didn't want to hear them, but there was no escaping those 1965 top ten hits that were now playing as oldies on AM radio. While everyone else was happy hearing them again and again, they nearly drove me into stage-three depression. I turned them off as fast as I could reach the radio dial; usually after the first three notes—all it took for me to recognize the song about to follow. And I tried to be fast enough to do it after two notes. I couldn't do it quickly enough.

I continued to wonder about Dianne: her job at the *Times*, her social life, her love life . . . did she have a lover? How deeply had she felt about me if she wouldn't make the effort to contact me? Did it mean it wasn't that deep, and she'd found new friends—or a friend—who had already completely obscured me? Did I exist in her thoughts?

I can't see my reflection in the waters
I can't speak the sounds that show no pain
I can't hear the echo of my footsteps
Or can't remember the sound of my own name

But I didn't try to contact her either. My pride was hurt and I had decided to try to wash her from my mind. I rationalized my stubbornness with the excuse that since she never joined in on any of Mary's calls to the Lamplighter group, she must have decided to cut herself off from them—and me. I'd dropped out of the Lamplighters, knowing they'd be asking me if I'd talked to her, wondering how I was feeling about her, what I was up to now . . . .

I couldn't face it. All I could do was try to close the door on her part of my life.

A year of misery straggled by, but I slowly managed to pull myself out of my self-made funk, finally finding a small amount of solace in my work and a little resurgence in my outlook with the new, emerging music scene. Dylan had blown the rock world away in '65 with the new sounds of his *Highway 61* and *Bringing it all Back Home* albums. The Beatles had responded by releasing three new albums that year, the Stones with two, and all three continued prolifically over the next several years with albums full of great music. The rock world was burning with new musical ideas and sounds. Thankfully it was impossible for me to stay in my black mood with that kind of creativity jumping out of my car's AM radio. The new music became my salvation.

As time went by, the pain of losing Dianne faded and I began to find people and interests to replace her. But not completely. I found myself comparing every new girl I met to Dianne's social awareness, political knowledge, music and theater interests, vibrant personality, and conversational skills. I had to stop. Trying to find a girl who would be my new Dianne was a path to nowhere: a mission impossible.

I started seeing a vision of myself as an old man in his last years, still single and beaten down by the knowledge he'd let the only one slip away, and had never managed to find that girl again. I had to get out of the hole I'd dug for myself.

Sara Wilson lifted me out. She was a Dayton girl who was open to out-of-towners. Out-of-towners who would fix a flat tire, that is. Although I was hardly an out-of-towner any longer; I'd been living in Dayton by then for nearly three years. Except for my times with Dianne, three lonely years until one day when I rounded a curve on a back road to Yellow Springs and nearly hit a Mustang sitting half on and half off the road. She was standing there in a pretty skirt, blouse, cardigan sweater, stockings, and heels, ready to cry, despair in her eyes as she stared disbelievingly at the flat left rear. She was trying to get to an interview and was probably going to be late. Late and dirty if she tried doing what her dad had shown her about changing tires on a roadway.

"Hi, looks like you need a little help."

"Oh, please! Yes, I need help. I can't change that tire even though Dad showed me how to do it. He wouldn't let me take my driver's test until I learned how to change tires. But I can't do it dressed like this and still get to my interview . . . ."

"I'll do it. Open the trunk for me, please."

Woo—ee! ride me high, tomorrow's the day, the bride's gonna come . . . .

Three kids, six dogs, four houses—all in Dayton—and twenty-one years later, I was a single man again. Sara had been a wonderful wife and life companion. She got that job, but the working world wasn't Sara's world. She was a mother, a teacher, a nature lover, my lover, and the wife of a lifetime. She'd been gone for over a year when I told the kids, now grown and living on their own, that I'd had a longtime wish to move to California and was going to go out there to try it out, before . . . .

Before what? I didn't have a clue. Before I got too old? Before I died? *Before Dianne—*

I didn't want to admit to myself that time wasn't on my side and I had to do it then— before time won out. I realized it had everything to do with trying to discover what Dianne and Mary and Pete must have discovered: what I had missed all those years ago.

"But Dad, we're your family. We're here! Why would you want to go out there and live alone?"

"Don't worry about me. I need some space and time for myself." I loved my kids, but truthfully, they were more Sara's kids than mine. I was on the road so much of the time that Sara was the one who raised them. She was a full-time mother and part-time father to two boys and one girl. At times, I felt more like an uncle than a father. And that may have been how they felt about me too: not quite a father, and more like a very close uncle. But Sara was wonderful about it. High paying, high-tech jobs like mine were scarce enough in Dayton and we both knew I had to do whatever it took to keep that job and maintain our home and lifestyle. She was happy enough to be able to raise the kids in a safe, stress-free environment and get them pointed in the right direction. And she was always there with open arms when I returned from wherever I'd been in my worldwide travels.

I told them I wouldn't sell my Dayton house. I'd rent a furnished place out there and give myself a year to figure out what I really wanted to do.

And why not? As Dianne had said, "You don't owe anyone anything; you don't want to miss out on this!"

Down deep, I always believed she was right.

And someday maybe, who knows, baby, I'll come and be cryin' to you . . . .

California Dreams

$\mathcal{I}$ spent weeks in the summer of 1990, before leaving for California, searching for information about Pete Allison and Mary James and Dianne
Wolfe. I wanted to at least have a decent idea of where I might find any of
them before beginning my four-day drive. If I could find one of them and get
a phone number, I'd be able talk to him or her and come up with a plan for
my trip and destination. I was open to anything at that point, but the better
weather, easier traffic, and lower population of San Diego attracted me. I hit
the wall at every turn. I came up with more wrong and out-of-service phone
numbers than I believed the phone companies would ever allow. What ever
happened to: "The new number is . . . ?"

I gave up on 411 searches and tried and exhausted all the resources I could
think of in the Dayton area. All three were from single child homes, with
most of the parents deceased. In Dianne's case, her still-living father, clearly
falling into dementia, told me he'd hung up on her until she stopped calling.
He said the last time he saw her they'd argued about how much he hated that
she was teaching at that "Commie" school over in Yellow Springs. He'd spent
his entire career in the US Air Force and couldn't understand why she wanted
to associate herself with the Pinko Commies over there.

That was before she left in 1967, and he said she'd never returned to visit
after that argument. The last he'd heard from her was that she was moving to
California. It wasn't clear to me if he really cared.

The few cousins of the three I'd managed to find didn't know anything
either. They hadn't heard of, or from, any of them for years. It seemed as if
they had been swept off the face of the earth. Of the few Lamplighter group

members I could find, now scattered around Ohio, no one had any contact with the three for years, and the old phone numbers they had were now out of service.

I knew that Allan Porsche in Santa Monica was the place where Pete had taken his first job when they arrived in California. But that was more than twenty years ago. There was little chance he'd still be there, but the dealership was still in business, now as Braden Porsche. I called to see if I could at least get a lead—a shot in the dark.

"Let me ask a few people," said the man who answered." Some of the guys have been here for close to that long."

After an extended wait, the office manager came back on the line, "John, one of our mechanics who worked here in the '60s when it was Allan Porsche says he remembers that Pete went to work at Shelby back in their final years. He says that after he left Braden himself to go to Hollywood Ferrari, he heard that Pete had returned to Braden when Shelby went out of business."

"Does he know anything else about him?"

"Only that when John came back to us from Ferrari a few years later, Pete was gone again and none of the guys in the shop knew anything about him. They're all pretty new here."

"I guess these guys move around a lot," I said. "Any suggestions?"

"Yes, that's the truth: wherever the business is hot. Well, Shelby is long gone, so you can't call them. But he gave me a couple of phone numbers for you to try. They're people who've stayed in contact with most of the Shelby team people."

But in trying them, I again ran into out-of-service lines, or lines never answered—"leave a message"—or dead ends. I kept the names and phone numbers for possible future use.

I was getting nowhere trying to find Pete, and tracing Mary was a non-starter. I never had a company name for that hot real estate development firm she had worked for, so it was impossible to develop a trail for her.

I could call the *LA Times* though.

"I'm sorry, we don't keep personnel records going back that far. And we can't give out personal contact information for current or past employees, even if we have it."

"I've checked your archives and see she was still there writing stories in the mid '70s. Can you connect me to anyone who also was there in the newsroom in that time?"

"Yes, I think so. But you must understand that they can't give that information to you either. That is, on company time or using company information. . . . The best I can do is transfer you to Tim Hartman who has been here since then. Good luck."

Tim Hartman confirmed that he worked with Dianne in the '70s, and he confirmed that he couldn't talk to me about her while at work. He proposed we have lunch if and when I got to California, though. And no, he wouldn't talk to me about Dianne over his home phone, but he would talk in person. And yes, he had run into her after she left the *Times*. The last time had been around five years back at an ex-*Times* people reunion.

So, after four weeks of trying, I had only two, mostly imaginary, leads: the possibility of tracking Pete down through the Shelby connections—if anyone would ever answer the phone— and the possibility of tracking Dianne down through Tim Hartman. But I did have the hopeful news that Dianne was, or had recently been, still alive and in circulation in California not too long ago.

It was all I needed. With that, I left for LA, Dylan reminding me: *The highway is for gamblers, better use your sense.*

He would accompany me all the way.

Questions

Four days on the road in my Jeep Grand Wagoneer with my entire collection of Dylan, The Beatles and The Stones—a mixture of newly released, remastered CDs and older cassettes—was still going to be a long trip. The drive would be close to forty on-the-road hours, not including gas stops, lunches, or just stretching the legs. At around ninety minutes per CD, I might be able to listen to all thirty of them without repeating any. While collectively these artists had published many more than thirty, my library of these artists cut off in the mid-seventies. The Beatles were gone after 1970, the Stones were in a lull for a long time during the mid-seventies, producing only one album every other year, and Dylan had gone into religious music and other styles then that didn't resonate with me. Or maybe I'd gone to some place where his music no longer touched me. I didn't know . . . . My last Dylan album was his 1979 release, *Slow Train Coming*. The thirty albums represented the heart of my mid-sixties to mid-seventies musical life.

As I drove and listened to the music playing on the after-market, cassette-CD player I'd fortunately installed before the trip, I was again trying to decipher Dylan lyrics, which had me thinking about Dianne. Except for occasionally needing to double-check my highway maps, she dominated my thinking. Was she still listening to music? To Dylan? *Good Lord, I hope she's not listening to rap, or heavy metal, or any of that other non-music.* I'd probably be able to handle it if she was listening to smooth jazz, but I hoped that wouldn't be the case. Maybe classical?

But what was it about this girl that captivated me so in that time? And then, more than twenty years later, what had me driving across the country to try to find her? Find her in thirty million Californians—if she was still in California? That she would be in California had always been my default assumption. But what if she'd moved to Oregon as many Californians had been doing recently? Or Washington, or Idaho?

No, I always believed I'd find her in somewhere in California; I never thought about it any other way. For more than twenty years, I'd pictured her on a beach, or a veranda with a beach view, or a mountain cabin with ski slopes in the background, not in a suburban neighborhood filled with bungalows and kids: not Dianne, she was far too cool for suburbia. Suburbia was for guys like me.

Find her . . . and then what?

I'd find her and we'd talk. Talk about her life; not so much about mine, which had been ordinary, but hers because I was sure that hers had to have been extraordinary. That would be after I hugged her and then hugged her again. I wanted to feel her in my arms. I wanted to feel her like I had that night in my apartment after our trip to Indiana. In my imagination, it was how I always visualized it happening; it couldn't be any other way. *Unless she's married. Then what?*

I wanted to know what she had experienced: What did she remember most? Who she was most influenced by? Who had she loved? Did she love someone now? And why did she leave? I wanted to hear it all. I wanted to consume it all. I wanted to consume her. . . .

She'd left before we even got started, and I'd always had a bitter-sad, dissatisfied sense of an unfulfilled relationship. I wanted to make up for all those years in one day. But I knew I also wanted more than one day with her.

For me, driving long distances had always been a great way of clearing my mind of little day-to-day annoyances. They disappear in the rearview mirror, opening my mind to bigger thoughts, issues I want to think about, rather than have to think about. With the open road in my windshield, I wanted to think over my responsibility to Sara. I had to try reconciling my present actions with my sense of loyalty and love. Should I have had a feeling of guilt in making the trip? Wasn't I being unfaithful to her?

I never believed in the concept of spirituality held by religions that insist a life force goes on after physical death, existing somehow alongside living people. Existing and even watching what we're doing? And sitting in some judgmental role over us? I believed that an ongoing spirit does exist—but as a mental composition embedded within the life experiences of surviving friends, relatives, and lovers. Not sitting on a cloud or up in space somewhere.

Sara's spirit lived on within me, our children, and the others who knew her. But spirits are memories only, not a quasi-physical or metaphysical existence needing to be satisfied with our actions. Imaginary conversations—debates— with spirits are inherently arguments with yourself, with the individual taking both sides. How can such debates ever come to any definitive conclusions? *She'd want me to do it. She'd hate me for doing it. She'd leave it up to me. Think of the children. Do what's best for you, dear. . . .*

I'll do what I need to do . . . . Help!

I couldn't reconcile my behavior in the context of my loyalty and love for Sara and our kids, and so I resolved to try to live with the conflict, knowing I'd never settle it in any permanent way. I'd re-analyze, re-rationalize, and re-judge it again and again. We do the best we can.

> *Good and bad, I define these terms*
> *Quite clear, no doubt, somehow*
> *Ah, but I was so much older then*
> *I'm younger than that now*

Sara was gone; nothing the doctors could do would have changed that. And morose longing wasn't going to change anything, either. Maybe my responsibility was to stay there in Dayton, in our last home that was now only a house; in that same town where my kids no longer lived, with me existing in the shadows of a vanished life. But I'd tried that for too long and it was a downer. I felt like I was doing penance for losing my life's love. Why did I have to do that? I didn't owe anyone anything, including my adult kids.

I imagined myself getting older by far more than one year with each passing year. I was living under a growing, menacing, grotesque shadow: age one arm reaching for me, loneliness another, and depression the ugly head. A shadow I needed to escape.

My escape was chasing a dream; the dream I desperately had begun to cling to; win or lose, right or wrong. Dianne probably never had the same dream, and maybe it would all be a silly annoyance to her: a middle-aged man chasing down an old girlfriend who'd moved so far beyond his experiences that there'd no longer be any common ground. But I had to find out.

I continued my drive with my new-found friend.

Connection

"So, Suze, let's talk about you."

"Okay, what do you want to know?"

"Why are you leaving home?"

"Oh, that. I figured that's where you'd want to start. Well, I can't stay back there. It's too boring and there's no future for me there. The place is all about farming, farming, and more farming."

"Why not go to college and find a career and new life after that," I asked.

"Mom and Dad aren't able to afford a real college. I went to a community college for a year, but it was a waste. The place was in a shopping center; a supermarket building made over to classrooms with an atmosphere that seemed like 13th and 14th grade high school classes. There was no sense of academia with a beer joint and laundromat on either side. So I dropped out and worked in a burger joint, saving up to pay for my tuition at a local nursing college. I'd been in nursing school for a little more than another year when I started seeing a guy, Danny, who was an old high school friend. It started getting to the point that he was the only person I was seeing since almost all my old friends had gone away to college or were married. He told me he wanted to marry me a little while ago."

"What happened? Did you turn him down?"

"Yeah. I figured if I married him I was going to be second place to his pickup truck. That truck was his life—his most important possession. All of his friends drive pickup trucks and that's all they talk about: which truck is better and which is faster; all that kind of guy stuff."

"I knew guys like that in Dayton. My son, the stock broker, drives a pick-up truck, but he never has anything in the back. It's spotless back there, like the rest of the truck."

"Well, Danny's a nice guy and pretty good looking, but I didn't really love him. I liked him, but not enough to marry him."

"I see what you mean. How long ago was this?"

"A few weeks ago, I told him I wasn't interested in getting married and settling down there. The only thing I saw, if I finished nursing school, was taking care of sick people all day and then coming home to take care of him and a bunch of kids all night. That and being stuck in a double-wide mobile home at the edge of town with him working construction when he could get it. And when he couldn't get work, or the weather was bad, he'd be in the trailer drinking beer, waiting for me to come home to 'entertain him' and complaining about this or that," she said, making quotation marks in the air. "And I knew I'd be pregnant a lot of the time—and the primary money earner all the time if I just let things play out his way. I'm not going to settle for that."

"I don't blame you. You probably would have felt trapped the day after the wedding. In rural areas, getting married and raising a family is supposed to be all a woman should want, but it's not for everyone. Situations like that can drive women into depression and drinking and drugs. If that's what they want, fine. But if they want something more, they should go for it. Women need to have their own lives."

"Tell me about it! There are more than a few cases of that in Salina. I have high school girlfriends who are already there. And to make things worse, all I was getting from my mom and dad was, 'You should be getting married.' I was tired of that argument; I have to get away now before we're fighting about it all the time."

"So, what do you expect to do in California?"

She gave an ironic laugh and said, "Probably flip burgers. At least to start earning some money and try to find a way to get ahead. Same as I'd be doing here, but at least I believe there'll be better opportunities out there."

"How are you going to live? Things are more expensive there than back in Kansas," I said as a sign welcomed us into Colorado. Eastern Colorado looked the same as western Kansas, but the dream of spotting the Rockies soon boosted our spirits after the long, boring hours spent driving through endless wheat fields.

"Aunt Julie said she'd let me stay with them for a while any time I wanted to come to California. It was a sort of open invitation. She said they have a big, four-bedroom house and no kids. Her husband Mike seemed okay with it, too. But he never says much; he's very quiet."

"Well, I'm sure you can charm him into submission if he's on the fence. By the way, do they know you're coming?"

"No, I haven't called them yet. I figured that if I called too soon, they'd try to talk me out of anything other than a short visit. Or even rat me out to my mom and dad, and that would totally be the end of it."

"Do you think they've read the note by now?"

"Probably."

"What do you think they'll do? Don't you think they're panicking, probably calling the police?"

"Probably. I don't know what they'll do. For sure they'll be talking to Danny to see if he's involved or knows anything."

"Did you tell him about your plans?"

"God, no! I didn't need him trying to change my mind. He'd take it as some kind of insult to his manhood and do who knows what. He's like too many macho-studly guys: girls aren't supposed to act on their own or have their own lives. I was an adult, living at home with my parents telling me what to do, and Danny trying to marry me so he could control me."

"I understand that, Suze, and I don't think I blame you. I'm worried though. They'll probably have the police put out a missing persons alert for you. If we get stopped for any kind of vehicle violation or anything, they'll have you and also be looking at me for aiding and abetting, or even kidnapping."

"There shouldn't be a problem. The note I left for them said that I'm leaving home and that I'd call them when I get to my destination and not to worry because they'll realize it's a safe place. But, I do understand that we don't want to get into a hassle with any police, so we'll need to be careful."

"Yes, like no speeding or wrong turns. But you have to promise me you'll call them as soon as we get to your relative's place in San Diego."

She was silent and looked uncomfortable with the conversation. But I wanted to know more. "Was living at home that bad?"

"No, it wasn't that bad—yet—but it was going to get worse. And that's not all of it. Part of it is the town and my situation back there that I mentioned. And it's partly that I want to try to find my real mom."

"Well, the mystery deepens! What's the story behind finding your real mom? Aren't the people you've been calling your mom and dad your real mom and dad?"

"I was adopted at birth. I wasn't supposed to know that, but I found out accidentally a couple of years ago. I asked my mom—my adoptive mom—about it. She started to cry but she told me it was true. We had a teary discussion about how she loved me as much as if she had given birth to me, and I do believe it. She said she'd signed an agreement to never tell me who my real birth mom was if I ever found out about this because it was a closed adoption."

"But why does this make you believe you'll find her in California? It's a huge place with thirty million people, and you don't even know her name, do you?"

"I hope my aunt Julie, once I'm out there, will help me with it. She's not all hung up over stuff like that."

"Do you think she knows who your real mom is?"

"I'm not sure, but I think she'll probably have ideas about what to do. She might even be able to get mom to tell her who my real mom is—if she knows. But I know that in closed adoptions, the families are not supposed to know anything about each other, but sometimes they do."

"I doubt that if your mom thinks it would mean she's going to lose you that she'd tell anyone anything about that. What makes you believe your real mother is in California?"

"A very old pediatric nurse I helped give home care to last year told me about her. She was kind of semi-delusional most of the time, talking about her memories and early family stories. When she asked my name I and told her it was Suze, and spelled it out for her, she said she remembered helping my birth doctor with my delivery. And she told me that she'd heard my real mother had pleaded for my new parents to name me Suze as part of the adoption agreement. I guess my mom and dad agreed to that because that's been my name all my life. But they didn't make it my first name; it's my middle name. My first name is Jennifer. I'm Jennifer Suze Arnold, but I go by Suze. My mom told me that sometime when I was between one and two years old, they thought Suze matched my personality better than Jennifer, so they started calling me Suze then."

"I think they made the right choice. I like Suze. I think it fits you better too."

"Why do you say that?"

"I don't know, maybe because I think of Jennifers as sort of soft and cuddly types while I think of Suzes as bold and adventuresome. But that's probably me stereotyping girl's names because of some that I've known."

"Did you ever personally know a Suze?"

"Well, not really. I do know a Susie—S-U-S-I-E—who is my daughter. It's actually Susan. After her fifteenth birthday, she didn't want to be Susie anymore. She'd decided she was all grown up then and wanted to be called Susan. You know how it is . . . . But I was in love with a Suze—that's with a Z—once."

"What? How could you be in love with someone you didn't know? Was it the same spelling?"

"Yes." I spelled it out: "S-U-Z-E".

"What happened? Where is she now?"

"Okay, let me explain. It was a fantasy. I never knew her; she was the girl on the cover of Dylan's '64 album, *The Free Wheeling Bob Dylan*. I just knew from looking at her in that picture, holding onto his arm and mushing through the snow of some Greenwich Village street that I'd love her if I actually knew her. It was an imaginary-love kind of thing. The kind of infatuation you can have when you're young, lonely, and looking for love."

I'm telling her everything about myself!

"I think that's cute. I'm picturing you all alone in Dayton, Ohio—in love with an imaginary lover. At what, twenty-two or twenty-three?"

"Twenty-three." *How did she guess that?*

"So why didn't you try to go find and meet her—follow your dreams?"

"Because I met Dianne. I guess Dianne became my Suze. And you know how that ended."

"Yes, I'm sorry for asking that. But what about your daughter, Susie—Susan? Tell me about her. Do I have to live up to certain expectations since I have the same—almost the same—name?"

"You already are, honey. Let's go back to your story about the old nurse."

"Okay. The last thing the old nurse told me before realizing she should stop talking about it was that she'd heard my real mother had gone to California after I was born and the adoption agreement had been finalized. She said she remembered me because I was the only Suze she'd ever helped come into the world. That, and how pretty my real mom was."

"That had to be a strange moment for you. How did you feel about it?"

"I wanted to cry. But I wanted to ask for more information. I wanted to make sure she wasn't making some mistake. But, like I said, she was semi-delusional and I couldn't get her to talk more about it. Her mind went off somewhere else and that's all I could get."

"That's too bad. So what did you do after that?"

"That was when I talked to Mom about it. And part of that conversation was when she told me about why they'd decided to call me Suze instead of Jennifer. She said they—Jean and Steve are their names by the way—decided that after some amount of time had gone by it was okay to start calling me Suze. Waiting for a while to do that would make sense if they didn't want to alert my original mom, if she was still around Salina, about me and where I lived."

"That's an interesting story, and you might be right about it. There is supposed to be a wall between the birth mother and the adopting parents in those arrangements. So did you know, before I mentioned the girl on the cover of Dylan's album, about that Suze?"

"I once read in a *Rolling Stone* article that Dylan's girlfriend in New York was named Suze Rotolo. I've always thought it was pretty cool to have the same name. Most people think it's the usual spelling, S-U-S-I-E, until they see or hear it spelled out. I kept the article just to show my friends someone famous who had the same name."

"Yes, well, unfortunately things didn't turn out so good for her."

"You mean about the baby that was aborted and then Joan Baez becoming his new lover?"

"Yes, and that she felt like Dylan was using her. She said she felt like one of his guitar strings to be plucked and strummed whenever he wanted a little amusement."

Don't my gal look fine, when she's comin' after me . . . .

"I know; that was all in the same article. I'll never let that happen to me. That's what I was thinking in getting away from Danny and his pickup truck and his ideas about marriage."

"But he didn't have anything to offer you, so it probably wasn't that hard for you. You have to be careful and very strong if you get involved with someone who has money or a high position; then it may not be so easy to walk away."

"Yes, I know, but I can handle it . . . I hope. I still have that article. I don't know why I saved it; maybe because I've always been interested in Dylan and the thing about my name and his girlfriend."

"I'd like to see it sometime. I only know the little I told you about their relationship. By the way, Suze, we're about to hit Denver and look for rooms for the night. How old are you?"

"Don't worry, I'm twenty-two. My birthday was last April. I waited until I'd saved enough money and I was over twenty-one to do this so I can legally be on my own."

"Okay, good. I don't want this to look like an adult man with an underage girl. And I don't know how to ask this in a way that probably won't worry you, but believe me, I'm not going to take advantage of you in any way: Do you have enough money to get your start in California?"

"I have two thousand dollars. It's in traveler's checks and a bank account with an ATM card. I don't know if that's enough, but all I can do is try."

"It's good to hear you've got something. But you can burn through that in a hurry if you're not careful."

She just gave me a sideways look that said, *I'm worried about that too, but I think I'm going to be okay. I hope . . . .*

"How does it feel, to be on your own—like a rolling stone?" I asked with a grin.

She laughed, "Ha, are you going to drop Dylan lines on me?"

"Whenever I can. I can never resist doing it when I have a line that fits the situation."

"Fair enough, I really like Dylan."

"You do? He's a full generation before you. The music is so different than your generation's."

"My generation's music sucks. There's no melody, no musicianship, no important meaning in most of it. And it's crude: Metallica, Guns and Roses, and Beastie Boys. Even stars like Michael Jackson don't do it for me."

"I know. I can't imagine singing that stuff in the shower, or letting it play on repeat in the back of my mind; you know, the way a song can get stuck in your head? But, are you saying that about today's female singers too?"

"There are some good ones with decent musicianship, but none of them have the vocal power and range that the girl singers from Dylan's early era had: Joan Baez, Linda Ronstadt, Aretha Franklin, Janis Joplin, and lots of others. Today's female singers, like Madonna and Cindy Lauper, are too breathy and mostly sing without power and that kind of emotion. And they don't really rock like Ronstadt and Aretha either. Today it's mostly about show: dancing in skimpy costumes with hordes of male dancers doing sexy moves, a lot of lip synching, and the vocal part is the least important part."

I was knocked out. "Yeah, I know what you're talking about! I'm liking you more all the time, Suze. So how did you come to these conclusions?"

"Mom had a box full of old VHS music tapes from TV shows like *The Midnight Special*, and *Don Kirshner's Rock Concerts*, and *PBS Soundstage* programs in a closet that I'd watch when no one was around the house. I put them on the player in the basement family room and watched them over and over again. I learned the songs and I'd sing along with them. I don't know; there's something in my DNA I guess that makes me connect with that music.

What about you? I can see you must like Dylan, but other than him, who were your favorites?"

"Jesus, I don't know where to start. You can't believe what it was like in the mid-'60s and the '70s. We'd been slowly drifting away from our parent's music: Dinah Shore, Patti Page, Perry Como and other boring singers, and—except for Frank Sinatra—we were done with them. But the late '50s and early '60s had a lot of what was called bubble-gum rock: silly music about Oh Johnny this and Oh Johnny that. Three chords, three stanzas and three minutes. Folk music was there to rescue us from the silly stuff, but folk still didn't rock yet. Then Dylan came along and changed it all. Even the Beatles, who were doing what I always considered bubble-gum rock in their earliest days, like "I Want to Hold Your Hand," realized Dylan's direction was where they had to go. The music had to say something."

"So, who did you like?"

"While everything was completely new and the upcoming bands were trying all kinds of stuff, I was open to it all. But the cream rose to the top pretty quickly: Dylan, The Stones, The Beatles, The Byrds, Hendrix, whoever Clapton was playing with. And then a little later, Santana and The Allman Brothers. I could go on forever, like Blood Sweat and Tears, and Chicago with their horn sections. There were a lot of one-hit wonders too that had great sounds but then couldn't keep putting it together, album after album. Quicksilver Messenger Service was one, Procul Harum was another."

"'Whiter Shade of Pale'! I love that song. But I've never figured out what all those lyrics mean. You sound like you're pretty up on that music, Mr. Patterson; do you understand it all? What's going on in 'Whiter Shade of Pale'?"

"Call me Tom, please. I understand it a little, but I can't claim I know everything that's happening in that song. But Dianne would be able to tell us. I'm starting to think another reason to find her is so she can decipher more of the old songs for me before I die."

"Sorry. Okay then, Tom it is. Ha, that would be funny: 'Hello Dianne, gosh it's been a long time. I drove out here from Ohio to ask you to tell me what *a whiter shade of pale* means.'"

"Hey, that's a better opening line than you realize."

"Do you still listen to music as much as you did when you were a young-er . . . sorry, in the past?"

"Yes, but it's mostly from the great years of rock. Disco pretty well killed my interest for a long time. But there are bands that kept going and kept the sounds alive and even introduced new sounds to the old. Steely Dan came along, so did The Eagles, and the Allman Brothers just kept getting better and better, even after Duane died. Same with Clapton; he just kept improving his musicianship and repertoire. That man must have literally a thousand songs in his book. So yes, I do still listen. I listen to the old stuff and I listen to the new stuff the old artists are doing."

"Like what?"

"Listen to what Clapton is doing these days. It's a mixture of traditional American blues, new songs he and other people have written, and his old music from Cream and Derick and the Dominos. It's an amazing repertoire. Same with the Allman Brothers; they just keep renewing themselves and their song book. And, if you think about it, you'll notice none of them jump around and hop all over the stage; they let their music speak for itself."

"I know, I think some of today's acts—I won't call them musicians—do that to hide the fact that they can't play. But you didn't mention Dylan in the music you're listening to now. Why is that?"

"Because I haven't been able to connect with the majority of what he's been doing for years, starting sometime after he came back from the motor-cycle accident. I was a huge fan during his solo acoustic years and into his early electric band days. I even saw him in 1965 in Cincinnati when he was on his first tour with his new electric rock-and-roll band."

"You did!"

"Yeah, third or fourth row seats. I was thrilled being so close to the guy who had created that music and was singing it to us. For the next ten years or so, I was still a huge fan, but after that, I began to disconnect. He changed in one way, I changed in another; what can I say? But, actually he's changed multiple times and I haven't been able to keep up with him. I feel a little guilty about that; it's always seemed I should have kept an open mind and changed my tastes with him. Maybe that's all part of my 'stuck in Dayton' persona?"

"No, I don't think that about you at all. I think you're a very modern guy and have just gone your own way. There's nothing wrong with that. Nothing lasts forever."

"There are things that should last forever, Suze."

"I suppose you're right. What do you think should last forever?"

"Dreams, good friendships, love."

"I like those."

"So don't forget them and always keep those in mind when you make decisions. You'll be happy you did at some point in the future. I'm not saying you have to stay at home and not go out into the world, but it's too easy when you're young to just walk away from something or someone, thinking it or he or she is replaceable."

She looked at me like I'd changed the subject. *I had.*

"You know, if we could ever get together wherever I'm living in a year or two, I could take you on a musical trip with my collection that I think you'd love."

"I would love it. We should make a pact between us to do it after I get settled down and can come to visit you."

"I think I'm liking you more all the time." I said again. "Okay, it's a pact. We'll swear to it."

She smiled a happy little smile and sat silently for the next thirty miles as we approached Denver, watching the Rockies growing bigger in the windshield.

What is it about this girl? It's like she knows me.

Colorado

*S*uze had asked me, for the second time, if I wanted to take her to the Greyhound station so she could try using her ticket to ride the rest of the way to San Diego. I told her that I was happy to have her companionship, but it was up to her. If she felt uncomfortable with me, she should go Greyhound and I'd take her to the station and wait while she made the arrangements.

"If you're okay with it, then I want to keep riding with you. I like you and feel good about how we're getting along."

Funny how that little, unpretentious answer made my heart sing

We left Denver in full sunlight with the air warm and summery after a night at a far-too air conditioned Ramada Inn with adjacent rooms, east of the city limits. As I drove, we talked easily about ourselves and common interests in music and social issues without any hang ups or worrying about what the other thought. I began to believe we were more in tune than I was with my own daughter. My kids never liked my music and were uncomfortable with my attitudes about life in the USA. They seemed too ready to go along with whatever was happening in current pop culture and their friends' political and social attitudes. Mainly they wanted to conform to the norms of the '80s and '90s. We were a close family, but we couldn't easily talk about those subjects. They didn't want to upset their girlfriends or boyfriends with debates over controversial matters. One son was indifferent to it all: my son the pick-up truck driving stockbroker, who didn't seem to have any convictions other than making money. They were good kids who didn't want to push the envelope in social matters. But how different was that from what most parents experienced with their children growing up in Dayton, Ohio? Suze seemed different.

⌒

She was in a long tee shirt, short shorts, and flip flops, with her hair pulled into a long pony tail. She slipped out of her flip flops and put her bare feet up on the Jeep's passenger side dash with her long, trim legs nearly straight out from her seat. She asked me if I minded her riding like that. I didn't mind.

We'd passed through the amazing views driving through the heart of the Rockies and down the western slope canyons where I-70 follows the Colorado River, raging and leaping alongside our Jeep as it dropped from the high country toward its meeting with the Sea of Cortez more than a thousand miles away. The highway flattened out, with the drive becoming more of an endurance test as we headed out of Grand Junction and toward Utah. Vista after vista of empty prairie with an occasional lonely, single mountain in the distance, dozens of miles away that, when passed, was replaced with another vista much like the last one. The miles slipped by that way; the Jeep, eating the distances at eighty miles an hour, rolled on, promising our arrival in California sometime late the next day.

We played CDs and cassettes from the box that was now on the rear seat, Suze pulling them out by the handful and sorting through them to find the next one to play. In a nod to my love of Dylan, *Highway 61 Revisited* was the first, followed by the Beatles' *Rubber Soul*. She started singing along with "Norwegian Wood" and sounded very good—every note on key and every syllable on beat. She caught me looking at her out of the corner of my eye and gave me a big smile, revealing no embarrassment or shyness, as if she were used to singing in front of people.

"Do you sing? I mean in groups or a band or with a choir?"

"No, just by myself along with the radio or those old VHS tapes."

"You seem so comfortable singing, like you've been doing it for a long time in front of people."

"I don't know why that is. I guess it just comes naturally to me. I sang in a glee club when I was in high school, and the church children's choir when I was in junior high, but I haven't done any since school. I'd love to sing in a band sometime, if I ever got the chance."

She sang the rest of *Rubber Soul*, and then all of *Abbey Road*, grinning madly through "Maxwell's Silver Hammer" and "Octopus's Garden." She was enjoying herself so much that, even with my off-key voice and hesitancy trying to hit the high notes, I joined in on some of my favorite tunes. We both laughed when I hit bad notes and muffed the lyrics. There were times we couldn't finish the song because we were laughing so hard. If I tried to finesse my way through after blowing a couple of notes in succession, she'd give me a sly, sideways glance and big smile that said my finesse hadn't fooled her, and we'd laugh harder. I was really starting to like this girl.

After several hours with my ears suffering from the volume levels Suze had cranked the knob up to, and my voice getting worse, I held my hand up and signaled her to turn the music lower.

"I'm going to take you directly to your aunt's house tomorrow, but only after you call her. You should do it today sometime to give her enough advance notice that she can be ready for you. We don't want to just drive up to her door with no warning and say, 'Here I am Aunt Julie'. They might not even be home. Do you have phone numbers for her so you can get her wherever she happens to be?"

"Of course, I have her work and home numbers. I told you I'd been planning this, didn't I? I wanted to wait until I was close before calling her so she wouldn't tell me to turn around and head for home."

"Okay, so look, we'll hit I-15 in Utah around the end of today's drive. That's where we leave I-70 and head southwest through Nevada and on to Southern California. So please make the call before that so you can tell her where we are and that we'll be arriving late tomorrow afternoon or early evening. I don't want to sound like a nagging parent, ordering you to do things, but I just want this to turn out well for you. You can use my car phone when you're ready, okay?"

"Okay, Tom. Hey, you know what I've been thinking is really cool?" Without waiting for my answer, she said, "We're both on a quest. You're trying to find an old girlfriend, and I'm trying to find my mom. And somehow, out of 300 million people, we've found each other on the way to California. It could finally be the 1967 you didn't have: rockin' and rollin' to California on a quest!"

A pain shot through my heart. It did feel a little like I was back in that time. But this time I was going, not staying behind . . . .

"I'm going to buy flowers for you to wear in your hair tomorrow, Suze."

She gave me another one of her happy little smiles—and turned the music back up, but not so loud this time. She sang as the empty desert and lonely mountains rolled by; cloudless skies creating the moods only driving through the American west can. So different from endless, flat corn and wheat fields and trucks and commerce everywhere. Using a little imagination, like this wasn't a 20th century freeway beneath my wheels, and those weren't jet plane contrails in the sky above, or that wasn't a fast-food, gas-station cluster surrounding the next intersection; we were in the old west most people still wanted it to be.

But the music on my Jeep's audio system and the young lady sitting next to me told a different story.

California

"Don't worry, he's a nice man. I'll see you late tomorrow afternoon!" Suze had called her Aunt Julie just after we hit I-15 and headed for Las Vegas. She said Julie wasn't all that surprised when she told her about being on her way to San Diego but became hesitant after hearing about her plan to temporarily live with them if they'd agree. But as she'd finished the call, it was clear that Julie seemed to have acquiesced to her plans.

"She's okay with it, but she's concerned about how Mike is going to react. She's not sure he's going to be happy having a third person living in the house because he's a very private person. He's not working anymore and mostly stays around the house now. But she promised not to call Mom—Jean—until we've talked things over and she's okay with my plan. I think it's all going to work out."

"Yes, but who do you think is boss in the house?"

"That's what worries me. I think Mike has final say on the big things in their house . . . ."

⌒

"Take the next exit and turn left. Go straight until you reach a dead end, turn right and then left at the first light. Follow Scripps Lake Drive to Mira Lago, and—"

"Okay, okay. Let me get through the next few turns and then give me the rest." I was more than tired. We'd driven all the way from Fort Cove, Utah where we'd had subpar motel rooms and a bad dinner and breakfast, and ten hours later were five minutes from completing Suze's trip to San Diego. I was having very mixed reactions over ending this phase of my trip. Suze had been a great companion for the last three days, and I was starting to miss her even before leaving her there. But it meant the next phase of my quest was about to start. It was both bittersweet and exciting. She'd provided an element of fun that I hadn't expected and I knew I would miss for a long while. She was one in a million—or 300 million.

But I was happy for her; I figured she'd do much better out here than she would have staying in the US's most central city—most central, and most isolated it seemed. I liked San Diego and believed it would be a good place for her to start her new life.

The meeting with Julie and Mike Baldwin was cordial enough at first. They both were friendly and seemed happy to see her. I was greeted warmly, but somewhat warily, and thanked for delivering Suze safely to them. But it was obvious there was a certain question in their minds about my provenance with her. While they were polite, their eyes and glances told me more: was this on the up and up? Did I treat her well? Did I keep my hands off her? Why would I have gone so far out of my way without expecting something in return? I wasn't going to mention that I'd paid for her rooms, against her wishes, before she went to check out. It wouldn't have helped the discussion.

"Suze, why didn't you take a bus or plane? I'm sure Mr. Patterson is a nice man, but what if he wasn't? What made you think riding with a stranger was a good idea? There are too many things that can happen to a young girl out on the highways, and almost all of them bad," Julie said, ignoring my presence. It was like I wasn't standing there.

"But I can take care of myself. Look at how it turned out for me."

"You are dammed lucky," Mike said. Then, looking directly at me, "She was lucky—wasn't she?"

It was phrased as a question rather than a statement needing my affirmation—not that she was lucky—but that nothing had happened to her—by me.

With both Julie and Mike watching me intently, other than trying to convince them I was a chaste Jesuit priest, the best answer I could give to ease their suspicions was, "Yes, I suppose so. Being picked up by a father of more than twenty years who has raised a daughter and two sons, all leading productive lives, probably was a stroke of luck," I pointedly answered, trying to ease his mind and put him off that line of thought.

He tried another line, "Do you know the chances you were taking, driving a young girl across state lines? You were probably breaking state laws all across the country," Mike said, again not really asking.

"Uncle Mike, I'm twenty-two. We didn't break any laws. And I'm going to get a refund for my ticket; I wanted to save money for getting started out here instead of spending too much of it on the trip. I don't want to run out of money before I get a job."

That logic seemed to appeal to Mike. He dropped the issue, looking happy to find an answer that worked for him. "Okay, I can understand that, I guess. It might be fun having a bright young girl like you around here for a while," he said with a toothy smile.

Other than questioning my behavior during the trip, he seemed to be happy with her arrival.

But as Suze told them of her plans to stay on in California and her hope that they would allow her to live temporarily with them until she found work and an apartment, things changed.

"Good God girl, I hope you know what you're doing. How do you expect me to explain this to your mom?" Aunt Julie asked.

"Don't worry, I left them a note explaining everything, and that I would contact them when I arrived at my destination. They'll know I'll be safe here and that you'll help me."

"We're going to be making that call pretty soon, Suze, or my sister is going to raise hell with me, too. They must be frantic. How many days has it been since you left?"

"This is the third day."

"And you haven't talked to them in all this time? Lordy, girl, I'd take a strap . . . ."

"I said in my letter that I'd be safe on the bus trip, and that they'd be happy to find out where I was when I got there and called them."

"Your mom's going to tell me to put you on a plane for Kansas yesterday. How am I supposed to tell her I'm not doing it?"

"If she says that, tell her I'll be gone before you can do it. I'm not going back. I'll tell her that when I make the call I promised. I think she'll under-stand—I hope!"

Julie seemed to realize it was useless pursuing it any longer at that point and just said, "We'll see . . . ."

Mike said, "I think it'll be all right. Welcome Suze, you're going to like it here."

Aunt Julie looked tensely at Uncle Mike again and said, "We'll see." Then she added, still looking at Mike, "But Mr. Patterson, before you head back to Ohio, whenever that is, check with us. You may have a passenger on the drive back."

They asked me to stay for a meal, or a cup of coffee and snack before I left, but I was anxious to get going. I needed to find a motel, a shower, a decent meal, and think over what had just happened over the last few days. I politely declined and went to the back of the Jeep to get the huge suitcase. As I lifted the monstrosity, I realized that it would have been a back-breaking trip for Suze if she'd had to lug that thing around by herself, ride to ride, motel to motel, or—park bench? I was happy to have helped her get here—but I also knew that with a little luck, she could have done it without me.

After lugging her case to the front door and struggling to fit it through the doorway, Suze stopped me and asked me to set it down there. While I said my goodbyes to Julie and Mike, she rummaged around in a side compart-ment of the suitcase and pulled something out. Then she smiled and hugged me, pressing her cheek against my chest followed by a kiss on my cheek with a delicacy and warmth that surprised me. I kissed her back, on her forehead. We were both getting a little teary and looked away from each other for a moment. From their smiles, it was clear that now Aunt Julie and Uncle Mike were satisfied that I had treated her well.

As I turned to leave, Suze handed me something folded into a neat square. It was a newspaper, beginning to yellow with age.

"It's a remembrance from me. Read it when you've got time to think back about our trip," she said, removing the flower I'd bought that morning from her hair and slipping it above my ear.

I hugged her and kissed her forehead again, "Remember we said we'll stay in touch. And remember our pact?"

"I do, and I will. Thank you, Tom. I do want to see you again. Maybe after you've completed your quest and I've made some progress on mine."

"Goodbye, sweetie. Call me if you ever need help. You've got my car phone number, right?"

"Yes, I do. Goodbye, Tom. Good luck finding Dianne." In a whisper, "Love you."

Love you. It was worth every extra mile, every extra penny, and every extra minute. She was a girl I would have been happy to have had as a daughter, or in a younger time, a girlfriend.

I exchanged phone numbers with Julie, shook hands with her and Mike, and turned to leave. But before I went out the door, Julie asked where I'd be for the next day or two.

"I'm going up to Los Angeles to see a man at the *LA Times* who remembered Dianne— the woman I'm out here trying to find—and had contact with her several years back. I'm starting with that lead and I'll have to see where it takes me. I'll probably be around LA for a couple of days." As I walked to the Jeep, I said, "And please take good care of my new friend." I waved goodbye to them as I pulled out of the driveway.

⌐⏌

A motel in Rancho Bernardo, ten miles up the freeway from Aunt Julie's, shouted at me from its sign far off the freeway. After a shower, room service food, and a beer, I was both tired and exhilarated. On the first day of the trip, I'd figured that when I finally arrived in California, I'd not only be exhausted from the drive, but also at least a little lost and confused with self-doubt about what I was doing. But instead, I found myself focused and happy. Suze was a breath of fresh air I'd been needing for a long time. And it was reassuring in that we'd found each other on our separate, improbable quests and took encouragement from one another. I knew we were both doing the right things for ourselves.

The folded newspaper she had given me in San Diego was tucked into an outside slot of my suitcase. With the last few sips of my beer waiting, I unfolded it to have a glance at her farewell gift.

"Dylan's Greenwich Village Girlfriend" was the title of the article. She had given me her prized copy of the *Rolling Stone* issue with the Suze Rotolo story as her remembrance. I was struck that after saving it all those years and keeping it as her personal connection, however faint, to the world of music celebrities, she had chosen to give it to me. What a sweetheart! I smelled the flower she'd returned and pictured her on that Kansas sidewalk.

Quickly scanning through the article, with a promise to read it completely in bed later, I found the author's sign-off at the end: "Story by Dianne Wolfson."

What? Wolf . . . son? Dianne Wolfson?

Traces One

"*Rolling Stone* editorial department," the voice on the telephone said. "What can I do for you?"

"I'd like to speak with one of your editors please. Are there any who've been there since 1985?"

"What's this about? The editors are very busy and seldom take non-business-related calls."

"My name is Tom Patterson. I'm interested in finding a Dianne Wolfson who wrote an article about Bob Dylan's Greenwich Village girlfriend in a 1985 issue of *Rolling Stone*."

"I wouldn't know who'd have any information about that. But I'm sorry, we can't give out contact information on any of our contributors anyway. You can understand they want their privacy and don't want to be deluged with calls and letters over something they've written."

"Can you give me any thoughts about how I'd go about finding her?"

"Not really. You might try other publications she's written for; maybe one of them will be willing to give you the information. But I can assure you that no one at our magazine is permitted to give out that information. Occasionally, some of our contributors do include email addresses with their work so they can be reached when they do want feedback. But if they don't, that means they don't want contact from the public."

It was time to call Tim at the *LA Times*.

"Hello, Tim? This is Tom Patterson, the guy who called you from Ohio a couple of weeks back. I called about Dianne Wolfe, remember?"

"Yes, I remember your call. Tell me what you're after again?"

"I'm looking for any information you can give me about her. She's an old Ohio friend I'm trying to get in touch with again, so I'm looking for contact information."

"Look, I have to be careful and protective of my friends and colleagues. There are people with long memories carrying grudges for years because they may not have liked an article written about them. That's why I told you I won't do this over the phone and we'll have to meet."

"Okay, where and when? I'm checked into a motel on Wilshire here in LA."

"It's too late to meet for lunch, so let's meet at my favorite Italian restaurant on Beverly Boulevard just past La Brea: The Trees. It's very near you; how about seven pm tonight?"

"She was one of the best young reporters I've ever seen come into the newsroom with so little experience. She had a nose for stories and how to get the details needed to print a compelling piece. And she wrote like a reporter with twenty years of experience: no bullshit, no fluff, no speculation, and no opinionating. She was going to be a real pro."

"Why do you say, *was going to be?*"

"She burned out. She told me the long hours and never-ending pressures finally got to her. That and her losing that friend."

"What friend? What happened?"

"The guy who got killed in a racing accident up north."

"Do you know his name?"

"I'm not sure. He wasn't a top driver. As I understand it, he was one of the mechanics on a Porsche dealership's team and was getting his first competition drives. Pete somebody, I think."

"Pete? Pete Allison? Was it Pete Allison?"

"Sounds like his name. There are other Allisons who are big names in the racing business, and I probably remember that name because it's the same."

"Do you know what happened?"

"I heard it was due to mechanical failure, but that's really stretching it. It's so long ago, I hate to say much more or I'm guessing. If you can find Dianne, she would be able to tell you a lot more. Why do you have this interest in Pete?"

"Pete was in our circle back in Ohio: a group of sports car lovers who got together every few weeks to tell stories and plan events. Dianne was in it too, although she didn't drive a sports car. She came out here with Pete and another girl, Mary. Mary and Pete were all but married, in every sense of the word except for the marriage license. I wonder how she is after Pete's death."

"I can't help you with any of that."

"But, Tim, what more can you tell me about Dianne? I really do need to find her."

"Okay, I'm comfortable enough now with you that I believe you really did know Dianne long ago. She told me the last time I saw her that she was living up north of Monterey at a seaside place called Sea Grass Estates."

"That's at least a start."

"Yes, but I don't have any phone numbers, apartment number, street name and number, or anything for you. Maybe you can get a phone number from the office up there."

"I'll try that. Thanks for this help, Tim."

"Happy to help. If you find her, remember me to her. Tell her I still think she would have been a star."

"I will. Thanks again."

"By the way, she did mention she had a girlfriend, or housemate living with her up there. But she never mentioned a name."

"That's good to know. Maybe it's Mary. One last question: I saw a *Rolling Stone* article written in '85 by a Dianne Wolfson. It was about Bob Dylan and his girlfriend when he was in Greenwich Village. The name seems almost too close to be coincidental. Did she ever write under a different name?"

"Could be. It's not unusual for writers to do that. Some have different names for different types of writing work—freelance articles, business brochures, event reporting, you name it. . . ."

I tried the Monterey area 411 operator multiple times, but if Dianne had a telephone, it was an unlisted number. I called the office at Sea Grass Estates but they said it was their policy to never give out names and contact information for any of their residents, or confirm or deny anyone's residency over the phone. Privacy was a major sales point in their contracts with the membership. The manager suggested that I drive up there and present myself at the gate.

"Why not give my car phone number to any Dianne Wolfe living there and ask her to call me," I asked

"That's the same thing as me telling you someone named Dianne Wolfe lives here."

I'd have to arrive in person, and if a Dianne Wolfe was in residence there, they'd call to announce my presence and ask if she wanted to let me into the complex.

Before driving more than 300 miles to Sea Grass Estates, I needed to find a better way to confirm what Tim had told me.

Traces Two

Ralph Stearly, a retired crew chief from forty years in big-time west coast auto racing—including the Shelby team—and one of the Shelby contacts I'd been given, finally answered my third call the next day.

"Sorry, my arthritis doesn't let me get to the phone fast enough these days. And I don't hurry either because it's usually some asshole robo-call trying to sell me something I don't need. What can I do for you, Mr. Patterson?"

"I've been trying to find a guy who I was told you once worked with at Shelby: Pete Allison."

"Well, I'm sorry to tell you that you are long too late for that. He died in a racin' accident a long time ago. It must have been back in the mid to late '70s."

"I heard that might have been the case when I talked to someone at the *LA Times* yesterday. But he wasn't certain. He thought he remembered the name but wasn't sure. That's why I've been trying to reach you or anyone who has been involved in keeping in touch with the old Shelby team."

"How did you know him?"

"He and I were in a sports car group back in Ohio in the '60s. He was the guy we all went to for mechanical advice on our cars. We all respected him for his knowledge and for being a good guy."

"Well, you can sure say that about him. Everyone on the Shelby team loved him. He was a great mechanic and was gettin' really good at setting cars up for races. He just got too ambitious about drivin' race cars."

"What do you mean?"

"He wanted to go faster than he knew how, is what I heard. After the Shelby team hit bad times when Ford pulled the plug, he went back to working on Porsches at the dealership he was with before Shelby. The dealership had a new owner who wanted to use the business to fund his racing hobby: Braden Porsche, they're still around up in Santa Monica. They agreed to let him work his way onto the driver's team, but they wanted him to go slow and run small bore classes first, do well there, and then if things were looking good, give him a shot in the faster cars."

"So, what happened?"

"He wanted to move up faster than that was going to let him. He started moonlighting, driving other faster cars in races Braden's team wasn't running. He got into a fast big-engine special owned by a not-so-first-class team one weekend up at Laguna Seca. All I know is that he either lost it or had a mechanical failure and went into the wall. It killed him."

"Jesus Christ!" I'm sad to hear that. I really liked him."

"Yeah, it's too bad. But racin's a tough game and the price of making a mistake can be your life. You talked to someone at the *Times*? Was it that beautiful gal from there who used to come to the races with Pete and his girl? I thought she left there."

"Dianne? Did . . . do you know Dianne?"

"I remember a couple of girls coming to the races to watch Shelby's Cobras, and then later, Braden's Porsche team when he was over there. Both were really pretty and a lot of fun. They'd usually come to the after-race parties that were always going on. One of them seemed closer to Pete than the other, but they all seemed really close to each other. I can't remember any names, though."

"Sounds like Mary and Dianne. They were a threesome back in Ohio and came out here together in '67. I'm trying to find the girls too."

"I really can't help. I don't know what happened to them. I did hear that one of them tried to kill herself a couple of years later but was saved by paramedics."

"Poor Mary; it was probably her. Pete was her high school sweetheart. They'd been a couple for close to twenty years when the accident happened, I'd guess. I wonder what happened to them . . . ."

"They might have turned out fine. There were a lot of rich guys hanging around the team in those days. They all bought high-end Porsches just to hang around with the team. A couple of them were friends of the guy who owned the dealership. They were always at the parties, trying to make out with the girls."

"Do you have any names or phone numbers for any of them?"

"Nah, I didn't like them: hanger-ons! Never liked any of them. We had plenty of guys like that hanging around the Shelby team, too, hoping to have a little of the glamor rub off on them, I guess. They had no clue about the hard work and sweat that went into getting the cars ready to race. They just wanted to be there for the partying and the press photographers—and the girls when the races were finished. Those two girls you named, Mary and Dianne, if they're the same ones from back then that I'm thinking of, man, they were hot. All those types were after them."

⸻

Hot! What did that mean? I wasn't sure I wanted to know. But the discussion with Ralph Stearly made me realize I should try to talk to the owner at Braden Porsche. Possibly he or others in the management team there were around the dealership and racing team in those days. There might be a chance one of them would remember Mary or Dianne, from the partying if nothing else. If, as Ralph seemed to be suggesting, one or both had become involved with any of the "hanger-ons," that information might become an important part of my search. It could lead to learning a little more about their lives. I didn't want to learn it that way, but I had to ask.

⸻

"Yes, the owner of the company is Ted Braden. His son, Paul, is the general manager. Why are you calling, please?"

She told me that the owner, Ted, had bought the dealership in 1970 and that his son Paul was now the general manager. Ted only came in one or two days each week. I asked when he'd be in next. After a two- or three-minute, nauseating, muzak-on-hold, version of "Blowing in the Wind" she came back on to say he'd be in the next day after ten am. She needed to have my name and reason for calling though before she'd schedule time with him.

"Tell him it's about Pete Allison and Dianne and Mary, and that I'd like to come to your place to speak with him about them."

"And who are they?"

"My friends from our days in Ohio. He should remember them."

⟵⟶

"So you are an old friend of Pete's from Ohio, you say?" Ted Braden looked skeptical.

"Yes. I've just found out that he died in a racing accident a long time ago. I understand it wasn't in one of your cars, and that he was apparently trying too much, too soon. Is that the case in your opinion?"

"Yes, that's always been my opinion. He could have been a good one—maybe even a great one. But he was too impatient. I think all the attention our main drivers were getting gave him a taste of the glamor and fame that top drivers get. He certainly wasn't doing it for money; he made more as our top mechanic than he ever would driving our cars."

"I'm sorry to hear it went to his head. I wouldn't have expected that from the Pete I knew in Ohio."

"Maybe that's what California can do. Especially here in LA. Stars get in your eyes."

"What about the girls who were his close friends? Do you remember a Mary and a Dianne?"

"Mary and Dianne! Yes, how could I forget? Two of the prettiest and smartest girls ever to grace a racetrack. Did you know them too?"

"Yes, we were all part of a group that sometimes did things together back in Ohio. Dianne and I were pretty good friends until she left to come out here. I was the guy left behind."

"Your bad luck, my friend. She was special."

"Did she become someone's, 'good luck' out here?"

"Not that I know. She seemed to love being around everything: the race team, the parties, the special guests we often had at the track parties and at our place. She was very popular with a set of people around Santa Monica and down in Newport Beach. You know, the chic crowd. But I believe she just did it for the social occasions, not gold digging. She and Mary always seemed to arrive and leave together. That is, until Pete's accident."

"What happened after that?"

"Mary stopped coming to the tracks and parties. Dianne still came to a race once in a while, and even showed up at some of the parties, but she always left early—alone as far as I could tell."

"When was the last contact you had with her?"

"I don't know. It seemed she just vanished, and I never saw her again. It might have been around the time she left the *Times*. I seem to recall not seeing her stories in the city section around the same time. Paul might know a little more. He wasn't busy running the business then and might have been more aware of her."

"Ask Paul to come in please, Jeanette," Ted asked his assistant.

A young man looking too youthful to be running a hugely successful Porsche dealership came into the room.

"Paul, this is Tom, from Ohio. He's an old friend of Pete Allison's and the two girlfriends who were always with him. You remember Mary and Dianne, right?"

"Hi Tom. Yes, yes, I remember them. Fun girls. I missed them when they dropped out of our little circle after Pete died."

"Tom's trying to find either, or both. Got any ideas on how he might do that?"

"Long time ago. I don't know . . . there was a guy from Santa Monica who was really making a push for the shorter one; I believe she was Mary. He used to hang around the tracks and find a way to get into the pits during the races, then stay around for the parties. He had a lot of bucks; his dad was a builder in the Malibu area: Ralph Carver; owned Carver Construction. The kid, Jim, was always parading around in the latest Ferrari, trying to score with girls on the racing scene. It surprised me anyone would give him the time of day because he was such a sham: all show and no go."

"So what happened with them?" I asked.

"Not sure. I saw them around the beach clubs and night clubs a few times in the next year or so. But after a while, no one seemed to see them around any longer. It was a funny thing; they were always a threesome. I never saw him with just one of the two; it was always both. People were wondering about the girl's sexual orientations—and Carver's too—because of that back then. But I wouldn't know; you'd have to ask Jim Carver about it."

"I'm don't think I want to ask him about that, but I would like to ask what he knows about where they might be. Do you have a phone number for him?"

"Just call Carver Construction. Jim's the owner now. But I should warn you, he's a real pain in the ass. He's going to hassle you about who you are and why you're calling, and why you want information—any information by the way. He's suspicious of everyone; always made me wonder what he might be hiding. And, on top of that, he's the most arrogant guy I've ever known. He can't stop bragging about himself."

"Sounds like a real charmer," I said.

"Yeah. Jesus, those girls must have been desperate—or broke—or both. He's got a scummy reputation these days."

Paul paged through a Yellow Pages phone book four inches thick. "Here's the number. Good luck—and don't tell him I told you to call."

Traces Three

"Jim Carver here. Who's this?"

"My name is Tom Patterson. I'm from Dayton, Ohio, and I'm trying to find old friends who came out here in the '60s."

"I don't know anyone from Dayton, Ohio," he said. I could see his sneer over the telephone connection.

"Well, maybe they never told you about being from Dayton, Ohio." Thinking I'd feed his arrogance, I added, "It's nothing to brag about."

"I can believe that! Cash registers? That's all they make there. I've always heard it's a shithole. What were their names?"

"Dianne Wolfe and Mary James."

"Oh, those girls! Yeah, I remember them a little. They kinda' hung around some of the racing people back in the '60s and '70s. Weren't very popular with the crowd out here. Like farm girls, ha-ha-ha. Kinda' square. What do you want and why do you think I know anything about them these days?"

"I talked to an old Shelby team guy, and he remembered seeing you with them a few times after Pete Allison died," I lied. "He gave me a few names to try, and you're one of them."

"Pete Allison! Now there's another name I haven't heard in a long time. Yeah, they were real close with him, especially the shorter one, if I remember correctly. He killed himself driving over his head and they were like nuns after that. I tried to lift them out of their funk for a while, but they didn't want to pull out of it and start having fun again. Losers!"

Gratuitously I said, "Well, I appreciate what you tried to do for them, it was good of you. What happened? Did you just gradually fade apart? Or did you find someone else?" I was feeding a braggart the opportunity to brag—a can't-miss strategy.

"Yeah, sort of. I knew there was something special going on between the two of them, so I tried to interest them in a little, you know, threesome kinda' thing? They needed help, I'll tell you that for sure. I'd find some joints and hash or 'ludes now and then; you know how it was in those days, right? Thought it might be just the thing to loosen them up a little and see what happened, you know?"

I gagged inside. "I guess so."

"Didn't work; nothing happened. Nothing except they got really pissed and threatened to call the cops and report an assault. I didn't give a shit; I had some pull downtown and just laughed at them. That's what I got for trying to help them."

Still gagging, but playing along, I asked, "What happened after that?"

"I walked. I didn't need the hassle from a couple of broads who didn't have a clue and were too square to take a little help. That was the last time I saw them. It was probably '75. If you're going to ask me where they are, or how to find them, don't. I wouldn't give them the dirt under my fingernails."

"Why do you feel so strongly about them? It doesn't seem like they really did anything wrong to you."

"They put me down. Nobody puts me down. No one refuses me when I'm trying to help them. I was good to them—took them everywhere, showed them everything, went to good restaurants, movies, concerts, you name it. Even gave them money when they needed it. I got nothin' in return. Why should I do them any favors? And why should I tell you anything? I've already spent too much time talking to you."

"Look, I have to reach them to give them some bad news about family matters. Wouldn't you want to help me with that?" I was making it up as I went along. Lying to this jerk wasn't going to be the worst thing that ever happened to him.

"Like what? Make it good . . . ."

"This is for real. They both lost a parent in the last couple of months. The families want them to know about it. The surviving parents and the aunts and uncles are all in their 80s now. I agreed to come out here to find and tell them," I lied. "You probably understand how that is. Aren't your parents in those years?"

The tone of his voice softened a little. "Look, the last thing I knew about them, a lot of years ago, was that they both were living together—nothing new there—up south of Santa Cruz on the beach in a place called Sea Grass Estates. I knew a lady who was friends with them and went up to see them now and then. She's dead now so I can't give you any more than that."

"Thanks. That should help me get started."

"No problem." Then, his voice softened a little more as he said, "Actually, they were okay gals, I was probably too hard on them with what I just said. If you find them, give them my best. And tell them no hard feelings; Jim Carver forgives them."

Nearly vomiting, I wanted to end the conversation fast. "Thanks, I will."

"Jim Carver never forgives anyone, but I'm doing it for them."

He really wasn't where it's at, after he took from you everything he could steal. . . .

Pacific Coast Highway

Ventura, Santa Barbara, San Luis Obispo, and Morro Bay all had passed beneath the Jeep's wheels before we rolled into the Big Sur area. I had been thinking over jerk Carver's comments about trying to loosen the girls up to have a little threesome with drugs. What a creep! I always knew that Dianne and Mary had a more-than-casual friendship going back to their high school and college days when they roomed together. I had seen the hand holding and kissing, but it always seemed right for them. There were obviously deep, sensitive feelings between them that, to me anyway, looked very natural. I didn't know if their friendship and intimacy extended to something sexual, and I frankly didn't care. What I saw was beautiful. I couldn't imagine it mutating into something like Carver had in mind. And that's what brought about the confrontation. Good for them.

But what even brought them to the point of hanging out with that asshole? I hoped it wasn't desperation over money and having to choose between him and living on the streets. It wasn't something I wanted to ask about; I told myself it was something I didn't need to know. In truth though, I did. How could it have come to that? But she'd have to bring it up; I couldn't.

Big Sur. The rolling central California headlands, covered with pines and redwoods, coastal oaks, and madrone. Gently rolling, wild grass-covered hillsides dropped to seaside cliffs with California's Highway 1 suspended and hanging over rocky beaches with huge boulders standing out to sea, like sentinels guarding the coastlines. Sara and I'd driven the PCH twice before when I had business trips in California, and we tacked a few days of sightseeing on at the end. We argued about who had to sit in the passenger seat, which, when we were southbound, was the seat nearest the coastal drop-offs, making everything for the passenger pucker up going around the scarier curves. She always won those arguments because I just wanted a happy companion in the car with me. The alternative was her screaming, "Watch it! You're going to miss the curve!" or "Slow down for God's sake; you're making me nervous!" or "Let's take the road that connects us over to Highway 101. I don't want to do this anymore." It was a far cry from driving through the billiard-table-flat landscape of western Ohio.

But it was okay when she got to drive. I could live with that because the rest of the time was perfect. Sara was the best traveling companion I could have hoped to have; she loved the sightseeing, doing the navigating, and planning where to eat or stay for the night. The drive through Big Sur remembering our travels together made me miss her more than I had for months.

As I drove on into Carmel, I gently placed Sara in my back pages and thought about Dylan living with Baez there for a few months in a cabin in Carmel Highlands. They wrote and sang music, made love, and dropped out for a while. They spent time with Joanie's sister, Mimi, and her lover, Richard Farina, who later lost his life in a motorcycle accident there. Jack Kerouac wrote the melancholy book *Big Sur* while there. Steinbeck wrote the vignettes in *Cannery Row* in Monterey and Big Sur. Beat poets and folkies of that era lived in the area, home to the Monterey Pop festivals of the mid '60s. And it was where I envisioned all the young people were heading when going to California was the rage back in the '60s: the Age of Aquarius . . . . The age I seemed to have missed.

Big Sur and San Francisco: girls with flowers in their hair, music every-where . . . and I had stayed in Dayton. If Sara were still alive, I wouldn't have been on this quest. How could it be that I was doing what I was doing—re-membering and loving the memory of my wife while also remembering and loving the memory of a girl I had known for only a few months more than twenty years in the past? I was in love with two memories, one now unreachable, the other possibly the same.

After far more than two thousand miles and several days of driving and thinking about it, I still couldn't reconcile what I was doing relative to what convention said I should be doing. But I drove on: past Carmel, Monterey, Moss Landing, and on to Sea Grass Estates. I couldn't help myself.

Reunion

*T*raffic barricades and a guardhouse finally ended my drive from Beverly Hills. The Sea Grass Estates gate guard, seeing I didn't have a remote control or gate code to let myself into the complex, leaned out of his door and asked who I was and who I wanted to visit.

"Dianne Wolfe, please. My name is Tom Patterson," I answered.

He showed no reaction at the mention of Dianne Wolfe's name but quickly looked through what seemed to be a small phone book. Watching me, he picked up the phone and placed a call, making me hopeful that this indeed was where she was living. In a second thought, I wondered if maybe he was calling the on-site manager to arrange an "interview" for me. I felt like an unwelcome intruder.

As I waited, I wondered what would have brought her here to this lonely, windblown coastal resort with the nearest upscale city, Monterey, at least thirty miles away. I knew from earlier visits to the Santa Cruz and Monterey Bay area of its fame for surfing beaches, but the coastal waters here were too cold for swimming and playing in the surf. And the constant sea breeze, while refreshing, can be too cold for anything more than brisk beach hikes. These beaches are more like Maine beaches than those in southern California: nice for looking at but not much use for swimming. Beaches north of Monterey are great for sitting indoors and watching the ocean with hot tea or a hot toddy, rather than playing in the water. What was Dianne after here, in this phase of her life; had she dropped out?

The guard's voice pulled me out of my musings when he asked for confirmation from the person on the other end of the line if he should allow a Mr. Tom Patterson into the property.

"He's sitting here in a car, at the gate."

"Are you from Dayton, Ohio?" he asked me.

"Yes, I'm that Tom Patterson." I answered.

"Yes mam, he says he's that Tom Patterson. Okay, I'll send him on through."

"Her place is at the far end of that row of homes, just past the parking lot. Number 101, it's the last one."

I parked in a sandy, windblown, mostly empty parking lot with scrub grass scattered throughout the sands surrounding the pavement. The nearly empty parking lot was evidence that Sea Grass Estates was a vacation-second home resort, with few permanent residents. I took a minute in the car to prepare myself for what was about to happen. My heart thumped in my ears, and I had a moment of panic, not knowing what I was going to say or how I was going to handle this reunion.

Who would be the Dianne I'd been searching to find for the past several months? What would a woman who'd left Ohio more than twenty years ago to live in LA going to be like now? I'd heard her and Mary called "hot" and "fun." That she'd run with a fast crowd from Santa Monica and Newport Beach. And that she and Mary had taken up with the creepy Jim Carver. Could I relate? Could she?

There was only one way to find out; it was intimidating in one moment— but heart pounding excitement in the next.

After a few deep breaths, with my heart still racing, I finally told myself to get a grip, and that a nearly fifty-year-old man shouldn't be nervous about simply meeting an old girlfriend. I stepped out of the Jeep and gathered myself, trying to look composed in case she was watching the parking lot from a window. I took on my most purposeful stride and walked toward the last home on the end of a row of ocean-breeze weathered, graying, wood-shingled, beach-facing salt-box houses. They all shared similar, but different in detail, cobbled, jumble-block modern architecture, separated from one another by small sand dunes and clumps of tall, sea-shore wild grasses. Despite their al-most abandoned look, located on prime beach-facing real estate, they had to be million-dollar homes. It looked like Dianne, or Mary, or both had done well for themselves.

I was still tense and full of self-doubt when I stepped onto the weather-beaten, splintered boardwalk leading to house number 101. How would I say hello to a woman I'd once been intimate with, held in tight embraces, and kissed? I'd felt the total touch of her body and inhaled the aromas of her breath, hair, and natural scents. Twenty-two years—*will there be a man with her?*

Maybe she'd be cold and sarcastic, say hello and we'd have our only con-versation on the doorstep, or maybe she'd invite me in and we'd sit at the kitchen table with the TV on, Dianne looking past my face at cable news. Or she'd offer me a bottle of water, saying, *you must be thirsty having driven all that way. Do you want another bottle for your return?*

And what would I say? Nothing clever came to mind now that the big moment was here. *Hi . . . ?*

She was waiting in the open doorway, one arm holding the door open and the other arm across her chest, hand on the opposite shoulder; her smile a mix-ture of welcome and surprise, and her entire face a question mark. Even after two decades, I could tell in a heartbeat this was Dianne: the same smile, the same full lips and friendly eyes, and still the same self-assured poise. "Tom, what a surprise!" She opened her arms for a polite, cheek to cheek embrace, our rigid bodies barely touching.

"Hello, Dianne. It's been a long time." *Weak, dummy . . . .*

I was taken with how pretty she still was, even then with the pronounced facial features that come with age: tiny crow's feet in the corners of her eyes and lips, little half circles under her eyes when she smiled, furrows on her fore-head, tiny skin puckers showing on her lovely neck. She had slightly graying hair, but it was still long, well below her shoulders just like she had in the '60s. As she turned, motioning for me to come in, I could see her hair was now a half and half mixture of fading black and soft gray that looked very fashion-able, beautifully swept into a barrette at the back of her neck, then flowing down her back. She was in a tee shirt and form-fitting jeans, barefooted—and looked elegant. And she still wore no makeup other than lipstick

"Come in, Tom. Come in and let's sit by the windows over there," she said, pointing to a room with a broad view of the sea and beaches. "You're looking well."

"You are looking wonderful," I said, accenting the "are."

"Thanks. I think living here by the sea has something to do with it. But you have to tell me what you're doing out here."

It felt very formal and stiff—not the room, but us.

"I'd love to. What a nice place!" *No TV with CNN on anywhere in sight!*

We walked into the large, modern room with wall-to-wall, floor-to-ceiling windows facing the Pacific. As we neared the windows, I turned to her as she was pointing to a small table and two chairs centered in the middle of the huge expanse of glass, where she'd already placed a bottle of wine in a cooler with two glasses. We stood there, face to face for a few seconds, saying nothing, a questioning look on her face. Instinctively I reached out to her, and just as instinctively, she opened her arms to me. In that moment, clearly, we both wanted that real embrace, one warm and with feeling instead of that first, awkward one. The hug at the door was just the polite thing, neither of us knowing what else to do. Through her welcoming smile, I had seen a slightly pale and tense face, revealing doubts in her mind. But now, relaxed and flush with warmth, her body felt soft in my arms. This was the familiar embrace I remembered and wanted: the perfect fit of our bodies, the dream I'd carried across the country.

She leaned her head back as we still held one another and asked again, "What are you doing out here? This is a long way from Dayton, Ohio. You have to tell me about yourself and why you're here."

"Where do I start? I came to find you. I've been on your trail for months now."

She leaned forward and kissed me on the cheek, eyes slyly half closed, "On my trail, why?"

"Because I had to find out about you: how you are, how you've been, what you've done, if you're married. And because I've always missed you."

"Missed me? That didn't have to happen you know," she said with a tight little wry smile.

"Yes, and how I knew it the day you left, and the next day, and month, and year . . . ."

"But why now, Tom? After all these years?"

"It was now or never. My wife Sara died two years ago, and I was just living until it was my time to die. I've always remembered you and wondered what I gave up that day I told you I wasn't coming. It's not that I didn't love Sara; I did. She was a wonderful wife in every way, and I've never regretted marrying her. But now she's gone and, I don't know, I . . . ."

I watched a shadow cross Dianne's face, "But don't worry, you're not on a bucket list!"

"Well, I'm glad to hear that! I'm sorry, I didn't mean about your wife, but that you're okay and not checking off little boxes. So now you're lonely and wondering about the girl that got away?"

"Look, I'm not trying to revive something that's probably a thing of the past. I just wanted to . . . to . . . to close the circle, maybe. I have this notion of unfinished business . . . no, not business but more like an incomplete relationship that I . . . at least . . . . Hell, I just wanted to see you again. I've never for . . . I've always had a warm . . . I don't know . . . you know . . . ."

She waited patiently for me to stop stammering and find a way to explain myself.

"Look, I've never had bad feelings about you because of your leaving. The truth is, my feelings for you have grown stronger in the past few years."

"Sounds like you're lonely, Tom."

"Do I? I guess I don't hide my feelings well. Lonely? Yes, I admit it. Standing here in front of you now; yes, lonely—and stupid: a grown man chasing down an old flame from his youth. You might even be married for all I know. Sounds like a bad soap, doesn't it?"

"I might not mind watching it; a good soap can be interesting—as long as it isn't over-acted," she said with another sly grin. "You are looking good, Tom. I remember you were a very nice-looking guy back in our Ohio days, and time has been good to you."

"I have to say the same about you. Beauty and wisdom both come with age? I promise not to get down on my hands and knees in our soap opera . . . ."

"Hands and knees would be getting too dramatic. And I'm not married, by the way."

I regained some confidence, "What, are all the men out here stupid?"

"Most of the ones I've met. I'm sorry you've lost your wife, Tom. Leaving you there in Dayton was the hardest thing I ever did—up to that time. I knew we could have a pretty good life back there. You had a good job, it was a good company, and we had fun friends. But it wasn't going to be enough for me in the long run. I've always had this belief that you only have one life, so you'd better give it all you've got. I told you that."

"I know. Maybe I should be sorry I settled for less than I could've probably accomplished if I came out here. Who knows what you and I might have done? But it looks like you did well." I pointed in a circle around my head, indicating the luxurious house. It felt like we'd never been away from each other. Our conversation was as natural and easy as it had been that first night I met her at the Lamplighter.

"Well, Mary and I did okay, but it was a struggle. I don't know that either of us would have been here without the other. Not quite what I imagined when we decided to come out here."

"Mary. Where is she? Is she here?"

"In the bedroom. She's sleeping. After she takes her medications, she sleeps for hours, or even the rest of the day."

"Medications? Is she okay?"

"She's dying, Tom. She has lung cancer and may only have a couple of weeks to live."

"Jesus, Dianne, I'm sorry to hear that. You two were always so close. It's going to be hard for you." It was the best I could manage to say.

"Closer than you probably know, Tom. And it is going to be hard. We've been close for over thirty years—since high school. I don't know what I'll do without her. She's always been there when I needed her."

"Can I see her? Is she well enough to see me and talk a little?"

"She's on an IV and has tubes in her nose for oxygen. She can barely breathe on her own and has medication constantly. Hospice nurses and home care aides visit every day. We can go in, but she's mostly incoherent."

We went into Mary's room for a quick glance. She lay in a hospital bed, tilted up at a 45-degree angle, in a deep sleep. I was shocked, looking at a person I only knew as a twenty-five-year old girl in the prime of life. Now she was pale, with gray-white skin, white hair, and bone-thin: a ghost of the person I remembered in miniskirts with a beaming smile and freckled nose, wearing bangs down to her eyebrows. We returned to the ocean view table where Dianne poured us each a glass of wine.

"I'm so sorry to be here at a time like this. Maybe I should leave and . . . ."

She stopped me, saying, "No, don't leave. It's nice to see you, and it's good to have you here. It will help me." She looked sad as she spoke in a whisper.

"I know this is a stupid question, but is there anything I can do to help?"

There was a long silence before she said, "Stay?"

"Stay? Here?"

"Yes. Here. With me."

"How long would you like me to stay?"

"I don't know." With a strange look, she continued, "At least until, Mary . . . hell Tom, forever might not be too long . . . . That was silly; I don't know. I haven't been able to think about anything farther out than the next day or two. I'm living a day at a time."

I stood and took a step to her chair, leaning forward to kiss her. We held the kiss for a long time, eyes opening in the last seconds; a flicker of . . . what . . . ? Love? Or just the old friendship? I wasn't sure, but it was full of warmth and gladness. It had come back like we'd never been apart—but also like we'd been apart for a lifetime.

"Are you serious? Do you have a place for me? Another bedroom?"

"Yes, I did mean it. There is another bedroom, but it's full of junk; you know, the spare-room syndrome? My bedroom is huge though and has two queen-size beds. You can use Mary's bed."

"Okay . . . do I have to stay in it? You stay on your side and I'll stay on mine?" I asked with a silly grin and wink.

She smiled cannily at me, without a hint of blush, "So you remember? That didn't last long, did it? For now, yes . . . probably . . . we'll see. While Mary's still here . . . I don't know."

"How would I forget? I'll do whatever you want."

"Tom, I can't . . . she was . . . we've . . . ."

"You don't have to explain." *I didn't want to ask.*

⟶

After hours of talking and nibbling on snacks Dianne kept bringing to the little table, and the sun long below the black-on-black Pacific horizon, she said, "I'm really happy you came to see me, but I get up early to check on Mary, so I'm tired now and need to go to bed. What about you?"

"Me too; it's been a long drive. How do you want to do this?"

"Stay here and watch the surf for fifteen or twenty minutes, if you will. You can come in then. There'll be extra towels for you on the edge of the tub. I'll still be awake, reading, and see you then," she said as she stood up from her chair.

"Okay. I'll go out to get my bag and make a call from my car phone to my daughter, Susan, while you're getting ready for bed."

With one hand on her hip and a smiling, sideways glance, she asked, "What are you going to tell her? That you're shacking up with an old flame?"

"Ha . . . probably not. I think I'll just tell her that I'm near Monterey and have found a place to stay for a while, and that I'll call back in a couple of days to fill her in."

"That's pretty good. Let's see where we are after those couple of days so you can give her a straight story . . . ." She left the sentence hanging there.

"Fair enough. I'm really happy I made this trip and have found you, Dianne."

"I can't believe you're here. And I can't believe how easy it has been to talk after all these years. It's almost like the old days . . . almost but not quite."

Then, with a serious look, she added, "There's a lot more we need to talk about." With that, she leaned toward me and gave me a soft kiss on the forehead before gathering up the things on the table.

> *Throw my ticket out the window*
> *Throw my suitcase out there, too*
> *Throw my troubles out the door*
> *I don't need them anymore*
> *'Cause tonight I'll be staying here with you*

Mary

"Mary, good morning. Someone's here. Do you remember Tom—from Dayton?"

Words slurring, eyes half closed, she replied, "Tom . . . Dayton . . . ? I don't know if . . . I remember a Tom who drove a little red . . . Italian car, but's it all sort of fuzzy nowadays."

"Hi Mary, Tom Patterson. I think you do remember me a little. I drove a red Alfa Romeo back then."

Her mind focused a little more and she looked at me with open eyes, "Tom; you're the one who we wanted along with us coming to California. I remember now. Wh . . . why . . . why didn't you come?"

"I don't have a good answer to that, Mary."

"You . . . you broke Dianne's heart, you know."

A twinge of pain shot through my chest. "I guess we broke each other's hearts then." Dianne looked at the floor, hands over her face.

"You know I'm sick, don't you? Did Dianne tell you I have cancer?"

"Yes, I know. I'm hoping the best for you."

She coughed. "The best isn't going to be enough. I'm dying. I think pretty soon . . . ."

I wanted to be positive. "I hope not. You've got to tell me about what you've been doing for the past twenty years. We'll need days and days to—"

"We don't have days and days. I don't think I have a week . . . . I don't know if I want this to go on even for a week," she said with a raspy, coughing voice.

"Do you know about Pete?" She asked, eyes dry and dead looking.

"I know a little. I'm sorry he was killed doing something he loved so much."

"I miss him, Tom. All these years later, I still miss him, every day . . . but I don't cry about it anymore; I can't cry. The doctor tells me my tear ducts don't work. What the hell, I can't even cry; I might as well die.

"Mary, don't talk like that," Dianne said.

"Tom, are you here for good? I mean, are you going to stay?"

"I don't know. I gave myself a year to come out here and see if I want to live in California . . . and try to find you—all three of you. I've wanted to do this for years . . . you know, catch up on what you've been doing out here, talk about what you're doing now, talk about our old times together. . . ."

"Well, I guess you only found the two of us, and pretty soon it'll be just one. But Dianne's always been the best one, so it won't be a wasted trip."

"No, Mary, it's not a wasted trip. I'm glad to have come when I did—"

Her laughing and coughing cut me off, "Yes, you're in time for my funeral."

"Mary, don't . . . please." Dianne touched her arm.

"Don't say that," I said.

"I know. I've got to stay positive. That's what everybody says."

Mary forced a little smile and drifted off before either of us could respond with more happy-faced encouragement. Dianne and I went for a long walk on the beach before being chased back to the living room couch by a high tide and strong surf, driving waves crashing onto the beach. We spent the rest of the day there, talking and watching the ocean.

"I remember you and Mary smoking cigarettes back in Ohio, like we all did. Do the doctors think that's what caused it?"

"What else would they think? But Mary and I both stopped smoking a little while after coming out here. I've stayed off them, but Mary relapsed after Pete's death. Actually, she hadn't stopped completely; she still smoked occasionally at parties and clubs, but she always smoked while Pete was racing."

"Nervousness while he was on the track?"

"Nervousness the entire weekend when he was racing: the Friday before, the Saturday of practice sessions, and the entire race-day."

"It sounds like she should have stayed away from the track."

"She tried that. But she said not being there and imagining the horrible things that could happen actually made it worse."

"She must have hated Pete's racing and what it was doing to her."

"No, actually she loved the entire racing scene. It excited her when Pete was on the track, dicing with the other drivers and passing cars. But it made her a nervous wreck. During a race, she chain-smoked, lighting the next one with the last one."

"Moth to flame . . . ."

"I guess so. And ever since his death, she smoked at least a pack a day."

"With you being an ex-smoker, it must have been difficult to put up with. Not just knowing what it was likely to do to her, but the constant smell of cigarette smoke."

"She was good about it. She never smoked in the house and we always kept a window open for fresh ocean air so it wouldn't settle in the house."

"Does she ever talk about regretting it: the smoking?"

"No, she only regrets losing Pete. She doesn't care what it's done to her. She says there's a million ways to die just innocently minding your own business; smoking is only one of those million."

"Yes, but the odds are far different with smoking."

"You can't tell a smoker that. They'll cite you some statistics about how many people catch lung cancer who never smoked. And it's the same story with race drivers: they'll tell you the odds of pedestrians being hit and killed by vehicles, and that more people are killed that way than die in racing accidents."

"Yes, people are going to believe what they want to believe," I said.

"I really think she's wanted to go for a long time," Dianne said, looking at a new set of waves crushing some teenagers on body boards.

Pete

"Tom, Mary's quite alert this morning; do you want to go in to talk with her? She's usually pretty good at this time, and then starts dropping off around the middle of the morning,"

'Yes, I want to see her." We both went into Mary's room to find her sitting upright, sipping tea that Dianne had made for her earlier.

In her weak, scratchy voice, Mary said, "Hi Tom. I'm sorry, I guess I dozed off on you yesterday. I'm more awake now and want to know about you. Tell me about what you've done for all those years. Did you stay in Dayton all that time? Did you ever get married and have a family? I want to hear all about you."

"Sure. Dianne's had to listen to all that for the past two days, but I'll be happy to tell you about my boring life in Ohio. I'm pretty good at the story now."

Dianne rolled her eyes and refilled Mary's tea cup before excusing herself with, "It's not so boring; make sure he tells you about his family."

After an hour spent telling Mary my story and answering her questions about my family and job, she started looking sleepy. I was getting ready to close the conversation when she said, with half open eyes, "Did Dianne tell you how I lost Pete?"

"Only that he'd had a fatal accident up here at Lagua Seca. I heard about it from a couple of your old acquaintances down in LA at the Porsche dealership, and a Shelby American guy who knew you three back in your LA days."

"I want to tell you about it, Tom. It's hard for me to talk about, so I haven't told people the story very often. But I do want to tell you about it because you knew Pete in our old days, and I know you'll understand it. Some people just can't imagine what drives men to race and don't want to hear about what they think is crazy shit."

"I know what you're saying, Mary. The thought of doing something like that causes a lot of people to just shut their minds. They can't imagine taking those kinds of risks."

"You probably know that he'd been working on the race cars, getting them ready for upcoming races, including some test driving."

"Yes, I knew that."

"Well, eventually Pete thought he could do better than the team drivers because he knew all about setting the cars up for the different tracks and was able to get the best out of the cars. He'd been able to show how fast he could be when he warmed the cars up for the drivers before the racing started. They could never match his lap times, so he figured he was ready to drive on the team."

"So why . . . wasn't that enough? For the car owner, I mean."

"He'd been driving some of the smaller cars and doing well, but the crew chiefs said he needed more experience in the faster cars than just being fast when he was all alone on the track. Winning races isn't just about doing fast practice laps; it's about passing and keeping from being passed with twenty other fast cars and drivers out there. Well, naturally, Pete knew that, and he realized that he had to find a way to learn faster. And that's what led to him moonlighting in other cars in different races."

"I can understand that. How did that lead to his accident?"

"I think he was in such a hurry to prove himself, he wasn't careful enough in choosing the cars and teams he drove for."

"What happened? Did he get into a junker, or a shitbox, as they call them?"

"No, I don't believe that was it. The theory I heard most was that the car had too much power. It was an older car that had been refitted with a very powerful, modern engine. I watched him in warm-ups in the car that day. He was sliding all over the track and seemed about to lose it at any time. I must have smoked a half of a pack of cigarettes in the thirty minutes he was out for practice."

Mary was having difficulty breathing and talking, so I interrupted her to let her catch her breath. "Take your time, we've got all day." I handed her the cup of water from her bed tray. "What happened when he came in after practice ended?"

She took a few small sips of water. "I'd never seen him looking like he did that day. He was sweating and red faced, shaking his head like he was thinking, 'No, no, no . . . !'" Mary shook her head from side to side, dragging her oxygen tubes across the pillow. "His hands were quivering so bad he even had trouble lighting a cigarette. And he had this strange kind of far-off look in his eyes that seemed as if he'd seen a ghost, or something that scared the hell out of him."

"He should have walked away."

"No kidding! But drivers are sometimes too proud to admit they can't handle a car. And then there was his need to prove himself; he probably let his ambition get the better of his judgment."

"If he was trying to win races to prove he was ready for the big-time cars, a ride like that probably was what he thought he needed. But I'm amazed Pete would have let himself get into that situation. He was always under control as I remember him."

"Yes, well this was LA and not Dayton. People behave differently out here. Anyway, he lost control of the car going down the Corkscrew—you know about the Corkscrew, don't you?"

The Corkscrew was, and still is, one of the most famous combinations of curves and elevation changes in all of auto racing. Starting at the end of a long, uphill straightway with a sharp left turn at the top, the track then drops steeply down a hillside while curving right and shoots the driver, tunnel like, into a sharp left turn. An oak tree grove on the hillside by the Corkscrew is a world-renowned spot for racing photographers and race action lovers.

"Yes, I know about the Corkscrew."

"I was watching the race from the oak grove. I saw Pete come down the short straightway leading into that sharp left-hander at the bottom of the hill and he seemed to be in trouble. He was yanking around on the steering wheel like he couldn't get it pointed correctly down the track. He was still sawing the wheel left and right when he came to the sharp left. The car went head on into the guardrail. It didn't look as though it had even started turning into the lefthander." She shook her head, closed her eyes, and took a long, slow, deep breath that made her cough.

"Take it slow Mary. I know it's hard for you to talk about it. You don't have to do this."

Mary opened her bloodshot eyes and looked directly at me, her voice a deep rattle. "Hard in more than one way: hard for me just to talk, and harder for me to talk about Pete. But I want to tell you everything."

"Okay dear. Just take your time. Do you think it was mechanical failure in the steering? Or maybe the brakes?"

"Tom, it's nice of you to call me dear. You don't know how good that sounds. Men with warmth have been too few and far between for a long time."

I held her hand, waiting for her to resume.

"The team inspected the car and said they couldn't find anything wrong with any of the components. But I never could understand how anyone can get a reliable answer when everything is smashed and twisted. The front end looked like a jumble of pretzels. And if it was a problem that was already there when they brought the car to the track, you know the car owner or the team members would never admit to bringing a car to the track that wasn't right."

"The guys at the Porsche dealership back in LA told me the car had a monster engine in it that they guessed had to have been too powerful for the rest of that old car. I guess you believe that theory too," I said.

"I do, Tom. He told me he'd never had to be so careful in any other car about getting back on the gas when exiting turns. It just wanted to spin the rear wheels and leave the track."

"That sounds like why he was having trouble getting it pointed straight after leaving the turn at the top of the Corkscrew. He may have lost traction accelerating away from the hairpin and never managed to get the car back under control all the way down the hill. I've seen that happen before," I said. I wanted to let her know that it wasn't uncommon for that to happen.

"That's probably the best theory. But it's not very acceptable, you know. Drivers never want to admit that a car has too much power for them. All they want is more power."

"Yeah, it's all machismo and bravery. But I'm still surprised to hear that it got to Pete. It must have crushed you, Mary," I said as gently as possible.

Mary whispered in a scratchy voice, "You'll never know, Tom, you'll never know how hard it was. He died in the hospital while I was holding his hand." A few tiny tears welled up in Mary's eyes and rolled down her cheeks as she squeezed her eyelids shut.

"I'm glad Dianne is here to be with you . . . is here for you."

"I have a request for you, Tom," she said, her eyes closed.

"What is it, Mary? I'll do anything I can."

"Opening her eyes and looking directly at me, her eyes red and now dry again, "Take care of Dianne. Stay here and be with her . . . after I'm gone."

I looked at Dianne, who had slipped back into the room and was already looking at me, "I . . . I . . . we have to talk about it."

"We'll talk about it, Mary," Dianne whispered.

That long black cloud is comin down . . . .

LA Story

*D*ianne and I had spent the next two days walking on the beach, talking—or sometimes not talking—or sitting on the sand and looking at the ocean and passing sea life. She arranged for a home care specialist to stay at the house with Mary when we went for lunch or dinner to funky little sea-side restaurants in Monterey and Santa Cruz. She showed me around Cannery Row in Monterey, the quaint streets of Carmel by the Sea, and we walked the boardwalk through the amusement park on the beach in Santa Cruz. Our conversations were mainly more the catch-up type: the little details of what she had done over the years; what I had done over the same years; family, careers, her writing, her dad who was her only remaining family; and comparing life in Ohio to life in California. She occasionally had to interrupt our conversations with long telephone calls involving new writing projects she was currently working on or negotiating. We didn't talk about Mary's request.

Sitting together on a love seat by the ocean-facing windows giving us a full north to south view of the coastline and Pacific, I asked, "Have you ever been back to Ohio?"

"A couple of times. Maybe ten years ago was the last time. I was on a trip to New York City to meet with a publisher, and on the return, I flew to Cleveland and rented a car for a side trip. I drove down to Oberlin first, then Columbus, and then Yellow Springs."

"A nostalgia trip?"

"I guess. I wanted to visit those places again. You know, let the old feelings come back."

"Did they?"

"Yes. But it made me feel more sad than happy. It was a very melancholy experience. I wanted to touch the places that started me off on becoming whoever it is that I am now. But my overall feelings were of unfinished things; strings that had been broken, words left unsaid, and people left behind," she said, looking away from me.

I couldn't ask if that meant me, but from the look in her eyes, I knew it did. And it would have been too hard to talk about. I shifted the conversation to a safer place. "You were so close; why didn't you come to Dayton?"

"I did. I went to see Dad . . . ."

"How'd that go?"

"I knocked. He opened the door, looked at me and said, 'I don't know you,' and closed the door."

"That had to hurt . . . what did you do?"

"He and I had parted on very bad terms back in 1967. We really didn't like each other anymore. But I knocked on the door again and he yelled at me to go away. That went on a couple more times with nothing changing, so I did go away."

"That's sad, but at least you tried."

"Yeah, I tried. But there wasn't anything there anymore. He always was a hard-ass, military type, and was getting worse."

"You were so close, why didn't you look me up, or call? I'd have loved to see you, or at least had a phone call."

"Tom, I knew you were married. I found that out years earlier, after Mary had talked to one of the Lamplighter girls who'd told her."

"But so what?"

"I thought it would be difficult for you and your wife. I mean, how would you explain me to her?"

"Just as an old friend from long ago. What's wrong with that?"

"I . . . I . . . can't explain it. I didn't want . . . it's complicated. Sometime we can . . . ."

"It would have been okay, Dianne."

She looked at me without speaking for a long time, and then finally said, "I had your phone number out, and the phone from my motel room night-stand in my hand, but I just couldn't re-open that door . . . ."

"My God, I've wanted to talk to you ever since you left Dayton, you know."

"I'm sorry, but I just couldn't do it. I knew it would either have to be some fluffy, meaningless conversation—that I would have hated—or we'd dredge up old, sad feelings, and I didn't want to do that either."

"I guess it's a good thing I didn't know. I'd probably have never made this trip knowing you were that close and decided not to call. It would have hurt too much." I didn't say *again*, but was thinking it."

She looked at me, and then looked away, saying, "There's enough hurt for everyone, I didn't want to add more."

We left it there. We'd been enjoying being together and didn't want to push ourselves into any sad places. After a short, silent period, watching waves rolling onto the beach, much like the effect of watching a fire in a fireplace, we found it easier to glide into another topic.

"Tell me how you found me, Tom."

"I talked to a guy down in LA who'd been with the Shelby racing team and remembered Pete. He told me that Pete had been killed up here at Laguna Seca, but he didn't have any details. From there I talked to the owner of the Porsche dealership, Ted Braden, who remembered you and Mary. His son, Paul, said he heard that you live up here but wasn't sure and referred me to a creepy guy named Jim Carver."

"Oh, Jesus Christ, Tom! You didn't talk to Carver, did you? Creepy is too good of a word for him! He should have been put away a long time ago."

"Yes, it was a little greasy talking to him. Luckily it was a phone call, so I didn't have to get close."

"Yes, lucky you. He always smelled of too much of a god-awful mixture of Old Spice, Binaca, liquor, and marijuana. He was revolting. But Mary and I had to put up with him for a while."

"Why?"

"We were broke. I'd left my *Times* job to start freelancing and had enough contacts and interest from different places that I knew I could make it. But I needed time. I needed at least a year to get projects going, completed, and paid. The real estate crash of the late '70s screwed us."

"How?"

"It cost Mary her job. We were depending on her income to carry us until my work started paying off, but the real estate market took care of that. Everything was turning to crap," she said with disgust.

"So how did that lead to Jim Carver?"

"His father was in the construction business and knew what was happening to people. He was a very good guy and was aware that people in the industry were going to be hurting, including Mary. He'd known Mary from the real estate development company where she'd been working, and from the racing crowd. He'd always been involved with Braden's team after having been Ted's frat brother in college at USC. I'd also met him during those times with Pete and the Braden racing team. We understood that he told his son, Jim, to check on Mary and me to see if he could do anything for us. That was like giving Jim a license to go wild. I guess he figured he'd be able to use his family money to 'help' us . . . and then some."

"And then some? I can imagine what that might mean, but . . . ?"

"Yeah, you probably guessed it: be his girlfriends. His 'chicks' when he wanted to go riding around Santa Monica on Sunday afternoons on Ocean Boulevard; past the clubs and restaurants and the amusement pier and down to Venice Beach or up and down Sunset Boulevard. It was all about showing off. He was a spoiled, rich-kid brat."

"But that's not so bad, if that's all it was about."

"But that wasn't what it was all about. He wanted more. At the end, he wanted a sex free-for-all—a three-for-all in bed. He'd been 'loaning'—his word—us money for several months to help us pay the rent and buy food. We hated taking money from him and made it clear there were to be no strings attached, and that we had no idea when we'd be able to pay it back. I was finally starting to get some regular money coming in from my freelancing, and

Mary's new job as a real estate agent in Santa Monica looked like it was about to start paying off. We were trying to get away from him as fast as possible and all we needed was for Mary to close a deal on an expensive property she had a lot of action on in Westwood. It was going into escrow and we only needed a few more weeks."

"But what happened? Couldn't you hold on longer?"

"No. You know how closing an escrow can be. Mary's big deal slipped a month or so, and we were flat broke and the rent was overdue. Carver wasn't so bad while it was just the Sunday drives and going to clubs on Sunset Boulevard. That part was actually fun; we went to the Troubadour and the Whisky a Go Go and saw all the great new bands and musicians, and even partied at some of their pads up in Laurel Canyon. But then he wanted the other things."

"So what happened? How did you deal with him?"

"He mostly had the hots for Mary. I guess he figured he'd start with her because she was really hurting after Pete's death and would be open to him. He totally misunderstood her, like he did everything. She didn't want to have anything to do with that. He tried to get forceful with her one night; she screamed at him, calling him every foul word she could think of and hit him with a table lamp."

"Jesus Christ!"

"It got worse. A few nights later, he came over saying he wanted to make peace, but it was really all about trying to get some chemicals in us. We smoked a joint with him and started feeling like we should forgive him when he brought out the hash. He smoked a little of it and tried to get us into it. We weren't having it and told him he should leave."

Dianne took a long breath before continuing, "We told him that we didn't want to have to deal with him getting stoned and unable to drive home. He smoked a little more, and that really set him off. He started making threats about having us busted for not repaying loans and a bunch of other stuff he was making up. He smoked more and got crazier. We tried to get him out of the apartment by walking him to the door, but he went berserk, hitting at us, screaming he would get us thrown out on the street and turn us into tramps.

Then he grabbed Mary by the throat and I lost it. I went to the kitchen, grabbed the biggest cast-iron skillet we had and hit him as hard as I could on the head. He went down like a blob of jelly and didn't move. He wasn't bleeding and seemed to be breathing okay, so we dragged him down the stairs and into the parking garage. We propped him up in the seat of his Ferrari and called 911 to report a probable drug overdose."

"What a mess; how did this all end?"

"He wanted to get us thrown in jail, but he didn't have a felony case against us since he was the one the police found, looking like he'd OD'd on drugs. He was incoherent and babbling nonsense. Later he threatened to sue us with a civil lawsuit for stealing money from him, but we all understood he was giving us the money with no strings attached. And there was nothing on paper, so it was his word against ours.

"Yeah, that wasn't going to go anywhere," I said.

"We threatened to sue him back for sexual assault and home invasion. I hinted at writing an expose on it under a fake name and publishing it in a sex-pose type rag. Finally, realizing this was going to be a disaster for everyone, Jim's dad stepped in and offered to find a way to settle things."

"And that's how we ended up here. We had a better legal case than he did, if it came to that. But it never did. His dad wanted to get it over with and settle out of court. We took him up on it and settled for a lot—to us—of money. After a while, when I started making good money from my freelancing and first novel, and Mary had made a pile of money from a couple of big real estate sales, together with the settlement money, we bought this place in a foreclosure sale and moved up here. We changed all the locks, put in a security system, got unlisted phone numbers, and warned the guards to never let Jim Carver on the property. We've been here ever since then."

"That was when, the late '70s? And he's never bothered you again?"

"Yes, that's it. Just Mary and me up here, since 1980. And we haven't seen his face again, thank God!"

"What a story. It sounds like it was a nightmare there for a while. But it seems that everything turned out okay?"

"That depends on how you define 'okay,' Tom. If you mean financially, yes it was okay. If you mean psychologically, no it wasn't. You never get over that kind of trauma. Not just the trauma with Carver, but the trauma of nearly losing everything and becoming dependent on a creep—any creep like that. We lost a lot of faith in people with that experience. We decided we didn't need to become dependent on men after that."

"By the way, he said he forgives you."

"Oh, fuck him! If anyone will be doing any forgiving it would be Mary and me. And we don't forgive him. Living here is a mixed bag. At times, it makes me think of him and remember dealing with his bullshit. I'm thankful for this place, but getting the down payment with what was essentially hush money bothers me sometimes—but not too much!"

"Wouldn't bother me a bit," I said.

"Weighing it all, if we—I—could afford it, I might move somewhere else. But I haven't been able to consider it with Mary . . . . Of course, there's always going to be his money in our equity, no matter how I'd do it. One thing is for sure though, I'd never give it back! But, who knows, maybe I'll think about it after Mary . . . . I don't know if I could live here alone."

Not knowing what to say in response, I asked, "So did the whole thing turn you off men? You said you never wanted to become dependent on men again."

"That's certainly true about arrogant, rich kid brats. But the truth is, neither Mary nor I have spent much time around men for the last few years. Together we've had all the companionship either of us needed."

"But his father was an okay guy, wasn't he?"

"Yes, but he was a mature man. I guess I should rephrase that by saying many men, especially egotistical, young guys that don't deserve what they have."

"I hope you didn't have the same experiences with other men, Dianne."

She looked away, silent for a moment, a pained look in her eyes. "No, I haven't. But I haven't let many get too close. There's another case where things didn't turn out all that well, but I don't want to talk about it tonight," she said with a tired smile.

"Bedtime? Same arrangements?"

"Yes, same arrangements; I can't . . . because . . . do I have to say it?"

"No. I'm sorry"

"You don't need to be sorry; I'm not offended, I'm just not ready for . . . ."

Kansas Story

I'd been up watching the gray fade from the ocean skies as the sun came up from behind Dianne's house, slowly chasing the overcast farther out to sea and replacing it with milky blue hues. Beach birds skittered across the sand while the tide was far out and the surf still gentle. A few walkers enjoyed the early morning peace of a Pacific Ocean sunrise. Dianne was up and placing breakfast things on a tray to bring to the table that faced the ocean through those huge windows.

"I love your place, Dianne." I said as she came to sit beside me after placing the tray on the little table.

"See what you missed all these years?"

"What, sleeping alone, across the room from you?"

"No, Tom! I'm talking about living in California—like this!

It seemed to be a combination of a slight jab, and a heartfelt wish-you'd-been-here-all-along comment.

"It wouldn't have been like this if I'd come. If I'd been here, things probably would have worked out differently. Who knows?"

"That wasn't fair of me. Of course it would all have been different."

"No Jim Carver, hopefully."

"I hope to God!"

"Maybe we'd have lived in some development in Riverside, raised four kids, and be babysitting grandkids now." I said, hoping to get a laugh.

"I don't think we'd still be married," she said, half sarcastically and looking very serious. But then, laughing, she added, "Who knows?

Different for sure, but I don't know how. I think we would have had fun. Don't you?"

"I do too. Yeah, fate. Who's to know?" But I knew she was dead serious about the Riverside idea.

"What's the point in talking about hypotheticals? It's unknowable. Let's talk about something else. What did you tell your daughter the other night? Did you tell her about me and our scandalous sleeping in the same room?"

"No, I told her I was looking at one year leases on beach condos in the Santa Cruz area."

"Don't you want her to know you've found an old flame?"

"She doesn't know I had an old flame. She probably thinks her mom is the only woman I ever knew. I never mentioned you to the family."

"I figured that out yesterday. I guess I'm a little disappointed. Why not?"

"I didn't think I could explain you . . . ."

"See! You do understand. But that's okay; I don't think I could explain myself to anyone either."

Wanting to change the subject, I said, "Okay. Tell me about the *LA Times* job. Tim, at the *Times,* told me he thought you'd burned out from the constant pressure of deadlines and never-ending six and seven day weeks. And, by the way, he said he believed you'd have been a great reporter if you'd stayed with it."

"Pressure? You don't know about pressure until you've—"

The hospice nurse's knocking on the side entry door interrupted us. Dianne went to greet her and escort her to Mary's room. I overheard her telling the nurse that when she'd looked in on her earlier, Mary seemed very bad, having slight spasms and trouble breathing. She stayed with the nurse for a long time before returning to join me

"She's getting worse by the day. Jesus, Tom, this is hell. Hell for both of us. She knows it's getting close, and I feel like my life has been in suspended animation for months now. It's so goddamn depressing."

"I know how you feel. You want it over, but you don't want it over because it means someone dear to you dies. Why does it have to be this way so often?" I asked, not expecting an answer to an unanswerable question.

Dianne looked sadly at me and said, "That's just the way it is. *'He not busy being born is busy dying.'* Remember that?"

"Yeah, from 'It's Alright Ma, (I'm Only Bleeding).' But does that fit? Here—for Mary?"

"Why not? I think it fits everyone, everywhere, anytime. You know there are 104 unique lines in that song, and that's the one people remember. And *'From the fool's gold mouthpiece the hollow horn, plays wasted words, proves to warn,'* precedes it. We're all just babbling anyway—that's another great line, but no one remembers it."

"I still don't see it."

"You don't really have to. Remember it's Dylan; make what you will of it. I told you that a long time ago."

"Yes, you did. And when I tried, you were in my face about it," I reminded her with a smile.

"Only when you were really off-base. But I've become much more forgiving about that in my later years; no use trying to be the best Dylan explainer. No one agrees anyway. What were we talking about before this?"

"The *Times.*"

"Oh, yes. Well, I did burn out. You have no idea what it's like when the editors want a story you don't have nailed down yet and they need it for the overnight print runs. I was always there, living at my desk, or out on the street trying to get the final details for a story. And when I did and had turned my story in, the editors were never satisfied, and I had to do edit after edit to make them happy and trim my copy to fit in the space they'd reserved. And that was before the copy desk got hold of it!"

"This was month after month, I guess?"

"Not quite month after month, but it was just about that bad. When big things were happening at city hall or during the election seasons, it was day after day. I decided I didn't want to spend the rest of my life like that. Fuck all those city politicians. I was sick of them and their flacks to the point that

I didn't want to talk to them in their phony interviews and press conferences. Ask a simple question and they answer a different one and take fifteen minutes to do it. It got to the point that they knew I didn't buy a thing they had to say, but I had to report it because that's what reporters have to do: report what they hear and see, not what they know. Fuck that! But I learned to add a little context and background that provided at least some objective perspective to what they said. A few tried to get me fired for doing that. Fuck them, too!

"How did you get out?"

"This shouldn't surprise you: rock and roll! I did a couple of low-level concert reviews for the entertainment department their regular critics couldn't cover that were well received. If they'd have asked me to make a transfer to that department, I would have done it in a heartbeat, and I'd probably still be there. But they had reviewers they were happy with and couldn't afford another full-time critic. I realized I wanted to do that kind of reporting a lot more than interviewing smarmy politicians, and if I had to do it by freelancing, that's what I'd do."

"That was a big gamble. What did you do to make it happen?"

"I just started calling around to newspapers that were a little too small to have their own reviewers. I volunteered to do reviews of music concerts on my own nickel with no guarantees. If they liked what I wrote, they'd pay me; if they didn't—my tough luck. I showed them the work I'd done for the *Times* so they understood what I could do, and that normally worked. So, I resigned from the *Times* and started freelancing for papers in the Central Valley, and some of the coastal city papers as well. It just took off from there. I even did work for the bigger papers like the *San Francisco Chronicle*, and the *San Jose Mercury that* had their own reviewers, but occasionally needed help. The *Times* even hired me back, now and then, for concerts they couldn't cover. I had on open agreement with them that gave them priority when they needed help."

"But was just doing concerts enough to make a living?"

"Marginally. When you look at the year-round concert tour schedule all over the state, there's a lot going on. But I need to be willing to travel, and have to be open to all kinds of music—some of which is pretty bad today."

"You weren't doing rap and metal, were you?"

"God no! I have my limits. My expertise is in certain genres, but not that. There's no way I want to even pretend to appreciate and review that form of . . . whatever; I can't call it music. I know that's career-limiting by the way. I realized I can't make a living off only dying music forms and had to adjust my principles somewhat to keep working," she said, pinching her nose. "But, I find myself doing less and less of it."

"So, what have you done about replacing it?"

"Write! I've written some novels and quite a few magazine pieces about the sixties and the hippie era–or as I like to call it, the time of the best music—ever."

"Like Dylan and his music?"

"You, of all people should know to ask me about that!"

"By the way, do you use a pen name? Dianne Wolfson, maybe?"

"Ha, did you find that one? I haven't used it for a long time."

"I have an old *Rolling Stone* article about Bob Dylan and Suze Rotolo written by a Dianne Wolfson. When I read the article, and saw the author's name, I wondered if it was a coincidence, being so close to your name, or if it might even have been written by you. I tried tracking whoever wrote that article by calling the *'Stone's* editorial department."

"Did they help you? Was that how you found me?"

"No, they are very protective of their writers and staff."

"I wrote that a long time ago—probably in the mid '80s. Is that when you started looking for me?"

"No, actually I just read it a few days ago. That was when I called the *'Stone.*"

"A few days ago! Where did you find that old issue?"

"I didn't find it. Someone who rode across most of the country with me had it. We'd been talking about Dylan a lot, and she gave it to me in appreciation for the ride."

"She?"

"Yeah, a nice kid. I'll tell you more about her later. She made me think about those times when we used to talk Dylan all night. Remember sitting in my apartment on Far Hills Avenue, drinking a cocktail or two, smoking a joint that you'd managed to lift somewhere and analyzing Dylan? I'll never forget them."

"Remember them? Silly, those are the nights that made me decide to ask you to come along to California. I thought we were born for each other."

There it was—maybe if she'd said it that way back then . . . .

"Born for each other! I understood that only after you'd left. By then it was too late, though. You know how it is; once you've made a decision, you have to defend it and you just get dug in. Christ, I was defending myself against myself! I hated it. I can't tell you how many times I second guessed myself, starting the hour you and Mary and Pete left Dayton, and then day after day after day."

"Well, I gave it my best shot, if you remember."

How do I answer that? She had given me everything.

"Well, here we are again, back to 'would it have been different?'" I said with a half laugh.

"I know, I'm sorry. It's the elephant in the room that's going to be over there, watching us and reminding us that sooner or later we'll have to talk about it all."

"I don't mind talking about it, Dianne. I've been telling myself for years now that if I ever got the chance to see you again, I'd want to do this. I want to hear everything about you since the last time we saw each other: what you've done in your life, where you've been, who you've loved, who you do love, how you are, what's in your future . . . and . . . how you feel about us."

"Jesus Tom, we'll need a year."

"I've got a year . . . or more."

"So do I . . . where do we start?"

"Start at the beginning. When you left Dayton."

"This is going to be hard, Tom. Hard for me, and for you," she said in a strange, shaky voice.

The nurse came in and asked Dianne to join her in Mary's bedroom. After a long conversation, Dianne escorted her to the door, arms around each other's waists, both looking gloomy. Dianne returned to the table, teary and red eyed, bringing fresh coffee, and sat quietly for several minutes before saying, "This could be Mary's last day. She's barely breathing and seems almost comatose. The nurse gave her morphine to keep her comfortable but thinks we may want to remove her oxygen and not drag it out. She said to think it over and let her know what I want to do. She'll come back if I decide to do it. Christ, I never wanted to have to make this decision for anybody. I hate it!"

"I know what it's like. I went through it with Sara two years ago." I reached over the table and placed my hand over her arm. We sat like that for a minute or two when I said, "We can drop that other conversation if you don't want to talk about it."

"No, I want to think and talk about something else for a while. And there is something I do want to tell you. Remember I told you that first day you were here there is more to talk about?"

"Yes, what is it?"

"I didn't come directly out to California with Mary and Pete. I dropped off the trip for a while to stay with relatives in Kansas."

"I heard about that from someone in the old Lamplighter group. You'd decided Pete and Mary should get themselves settled first and you'd join them in a few weeks to make things less complicated. Wasn't that it?"

"Partly. I stayed with my aunt and uncle there, but not for that reason."

"Must have been some great relatives to have made you postpone your dream trip. Kansas? I thought I was still in Ohio when I went through there!"

"This is the hard part. Not great relatives, Tom. It was because I was pregnant. I was going to have a baby in a few months and I didn't want to have to deal with that on my own, with a new job, and be in Mary and Pete's way with a new baby."

I was dumfounded—and humbled, considering what she had to be trying to cope with: starting off on the journey of a lifetime only to find out that she was going to have a baby.

"My God, Dianne. What did you do?"

"I was a little under two months pregnant when I found out. It was on the trip. I was due to have my period starting a few days before we left, but I was late. I'd missed my period the month before, but assumed—hoped—it was a fluke; that's happened occasionally. I asked Pete to stop in a little city in Kansas where my aunt and uncle lived so I could go to a clinic there. We stayed for a day until we got the results, which were positive. I hoped that I'd be able to live with Aunt Marsha and Uncle Harold while I decided what to do, or came to term there, if they'd agree."

I was full of questions that I didn't want to ask: *who, where, and when?* I side-stepped, "So that's the real story. I always thought it was a little strange for you to drop off the trip for Mary and Pete's sake. You were too much into going to California to just abandon it like that. I wanted to ask you about it, but you never called like you'd promised. I didn't know what to think."

The answer to those unasked questions hit me square in the face.

"Tom, she was our baby."

"Our baby! Jesus, Dianne . . . . But, just that once . . . that weekend?" The thought of those occasional weekends when she'd been mysteriously out of touch back in our Dayton days flashed into my mind, but, ashamed, I pushed it back.

"That's all it takes. And you had to be the one."

I didn't doubt her. If anything, I'd always known Dianne to be honest—even brutally honest at times. But what were those missing weekends all about? That question would have to wait, and didn't seem important at the time.

"I had no idea. If you'd called, I would have—"

She cut me off. "Would have what? Come to Kansas to take me home to Dayton? That was the scenario I was getting away from. I couldn't make myself do that, even though I wanted desperately for you to be there to help raise our baby. Going on to California and having the baby there didn't make sense: working in a new job—or maybe not working in any job and no income—and living where? A sleazy, cheap motel? And I didn't believe you'd ever quit that precious job of yours to come with us because of the baby. I'm sorry, Tom, I don't mean to criticize you. I don't have bad feelings for you over it; I never did and I'm not going to start now."

"But you never gave me the chance to do anything."

"I know; it's my fault, not yours. It was my idea to stay at your apartment in the first place."

"No. No recriminations please, Dianne. I loved it. That weekend with you is one of my most cherished memories. Even though it probably sounds phony now, I just wish I had been there with you. Tell me about the baby, please."

She was silent for a moment, gathering her thoughts and obviously choking back emotions. "I stayed in Kansas until she was born. I'd arranged for an immediate adoption." Dianne struggled through tears to say, "She was a happy, healthy, seven-pound girl with a mop of hair," before breaking down completely.

I sat there stupidly, mute like a statue, waiting for her to compose herself before asking, "Do you know anything about her after that?'

Dianne gathered herself, wiped her eyes, swallowing hard, and answered, "No, the rules were that you never get to know the adopting parent's names, home address—anything about them. I did see information about their backgrounds—jobs, and ethnicity and so on. So she came into my life and then left, all in a just a few hours. It was so sad; in different circumstances, Suze would have been perfect for me—for us."

"Susie? Did you get to name her?"

"I named her before she was born and asked that the adopting parents keep the name. I don't know if they did or not, but I've always hoped so. I used an unusual spelling of the name in the dream that someday, somehow, in better circumstances I'd happen across a Suze, you know, S-U-Z-E, from Kansas. I've always thought about and remembered her as Suze."

"S-U-Z-E! Is that the spelling?" I asked.

"Yes, you know where that name came from, don't you?"

"Of course I do. The girl on the cover of *The Freewheeling Bob Dylan* album. I think I may have just driven across country with her."

"What does that mean; you may have just dri—"

There was a soft, barely legible voice coming from Mary's room, "Tom, Tom . . . ."

We both walked quickly into Mary's room. She asked Dianne to leave so she could have a private word with me. Dianne glanced worriedly at me as she walked out.

"Tom, remember what I asked you to do?"

"Stay here with Dianne, after . . . ."

"Yes, after I'm gone. I owe her so much, Tom. She gave up too much for me."

"How would that help? Are you worried about her and what she'll do after . . . ?" I couldn't bring myself to say, *after you are dead*.

In a voice that was almost a whisper, Mary said, "No. It's that she gave up a man she loved for me. I'd tried to kill myself, more than once, after Pete's accident. After the second time, Dianne was having a falling out with him and decided she couldn't deal with him and me at the same time. She chose to help me by moving us up here to Sea Grass."

"To get away from him?"

"Yes . . . and no. I was always able to stabilize myself up here . . . . I guess it's something about the ocean and the openness." Her voice became weaker and more uncertain. "I . . . I could get away from all the people who knew Pete and wanted to be sympathetic. And I could get away from the rat race of my job." After another silence, she added, "I think Dianne wanted to move mostly for that reason, but it probably was to get some space away from Dave, the guy she loved but had the falling out with."

"Why do you think I would be the right person for her?"

"Because she would bring you up now and then, when we were talking about our lives. She always said that you were probably the best man she ever knew."

I felt numb. I couldn't even process the words; how could we have let it happen? Two people in love who couldn't communicate it to each other? Was it all just retrospective: more than twenty years of life needing to go by before the realization? Why do we seem to find some things out only when we've had other experiences, but the opportunity is gone by then? I thought again about what I had told Suze.

I had been speechless for what seemed like a long time but it was only a few seconds. "I don't know what to say, Mary; I can't promise you that. I have no idea how she's thinking. But I'll talk to her about it. I think I'd want to do it, though, if . . . ."

"Talk to her about it, Tom. Promise me you'll talk to her."

"I promise."

In a choking, ragged voice, Mary said, "G . . . good. I'm glad I got the chance to talk to you before I go, Tom. Please, I need to rest now . . . ."

She drifted away before finishing.

There's a long black cloud comin' down . . . .

⌒

Mary passed away later that day, never waking from the sleep she found after our conversation. Dianne was with her, holding her hand when she breathed her last, coughing breath.

Realization

The hospice nurse disconnected the tubes and straightened the bed clothing, leaving Mary lying at peace. The nurse said she'd call the mortuary service, Mary's doctor, and the county coroner to spare Dianne of all that; and she'd wait until the coroner and mortician arrived to let them take it from there. We held each other for a long while, standing by Mary's bedside with Dianne crying and shivering against me. I couldn't speak, knowing there's little to be said at a time like that. Everything I managed to mutter was nothing more than well meaning but meaningless cooing. But cooing can be important.

"I'm so glad you're here, Tom. I don't think I could handle it by myself. Thank you for being here. Thank you for being crazy enough to drive all that way in the belief you would find me. Thank you for your dreams," she said with her head against my chest.

We hadn't talked about my final conversation with Mary yet, although her questioning eyes told me she wanted to hear about it.

It was late afternoon when Mary's body was removed to the crematorium by the mortician, and we found ourselves alone again, sitting at the little table watching the earliest changes in the sky signaling the beginning of another Pacific sunset. In the distance, the early evening marine layer was forming as a low darkness far out on the horizon. The waves were quieting down as the onshore wind currents eased, allowing the waves to form perfect, rolling curls without choppiness and windblown spray. There was a newly opened bottle of wine, two glasses and a wedge of cheese with pears and grapes on the table. There was a lot needing to be talked about.

"What do you mean, you may have just driven across country with Suze?"

"Was your stay with your aunt and uncle in a small Kansas city named Salina, by any chance?"

"Yes . . . ?"

"Suze would be twenty-two now?"

"Yes, Twenty-two."

I told her about staying overnight in Salina, Kansas, and finding the young woman who'd fallen near the bus station—that I helped her gather up her things and then ended up offering her a ride to California when she couldn't recover her bus connections.

Dianne was now watching me intently, with unblinking eyes. "You just pick up young ladies and drive them across the country? Just like that? But, okay, you're a good guy—so?"

"She told me her name was Suze." I spelled it out for her: "S-U-Z-E."

"You're kidding . . . Suze?"

"She told me she had been adopted at childbirth and was going to look for her real mom in California. She didn't know her name or anything about her other than that her birth nurse told her a few years ago that she'd heard her mom had moved to California a few weeks after she was born."

"My baby . . . ? Our baby! I don't believe this."

"She's the girl who gave me the *Rolling Stone* article. She had saved it because of her fascination with her own name and Dylan's girlfriend's name being the same."

"You're telling me my—our—daughter just rode across the country with you? Where is she now?"

"She's in San Diego. I took her to her aunt's place there, and she hopes to stay with her until she gets a job and can live on her own. And she wants to look for you."

"Oh, my God! I want to see her. I want to hold and kiss her. I've got to see her; help me please," Dianne said with tears filling her eyes, both hands gripping my arm.

"I know. I want to see her again too. But this time I'll see her as my daughter! There was always something about her that seemed so familiar, so easy to be with . . . . You're going to love her, Dianne."

Dianne fought back tears and regained her voice. "This is incredible, I can't wait! But first we have to take care of Mary."

"Yes, I'll help you any way I can."

"My God Tom, how did you find me just when I needed someone? I have to tell you again how glad I am that you came to find me and that you're here."

"Better late than never?"

"1967 wouldn't have been too soon, Tom . . . ."

"I know. But at least I brought your—our—daughter along."

"Please call her and tell her you have someone who wants to meet her."

⌒⟶

Mary, with Dianne's help, had pre-arranged for a next-day cremation after her death and to have her ashes buried at sea. Dianne called Mary's few friends to invite them over for a memorial get-together the next day. I arranged for a boat-for-hire service to sail us offshore to scatter Mary's ashes over the water a few miles directly out from the house.

> *Yes, to dance beneath the diamond sky with one hand waving free*
> *Silhouetted by the sea, circled by the circus sands*
> *With all memory and fate driven deep beneath the waves*
> *Let me forget about today until tomorrow*

I called Julie and Mike's number in San Diego but had to leave a message on their answering machine, asking for Suze, or for anyone there to call me at Dianne's home number.

Guilt

ary's memorial was a simple get together with Dianne, myself, and a few people from the resort-HOA Mary had worked closely with as director of operations for several years in attendance. We spent the early evening hours on the ocean-facing patio deck quietly talking about memories of Mary, with wine, champagne, coffee and snacks until the sun dropped behind the evening clouds, leaving us in a chilly breeze. Earlier in the day, Dianne and I had sailed with the boat captain out to sea where Dianne scattered Mary's ashes over the water. The boat captain, seabirds, and I had been the only witnesses to Dianne and Mary's final caress as she poured Mary's ashes into the sea, sadly sifting them through her farewell-wishing free hand, as they were scattered over the surface by the fresh sea-breeze.

With the guests finally gone, we sat together in one of the paired love seats watching a gently glowing fire in the free-standing fireplace. Moonlit, foam-covered, small waves, sparkling against the dark ocean, were breaking on the beach with a gentle, whispering murmur.

"Please call Suze's relative's number in San Diego again so we can talk to her and arrange to meet. It's been a day and a half now and we still haven't heard from them."

"Sure, but let's figure out how we do this. Do you want me to talk to her first and tell her about you? And do I just hit her up front with the fact that we are her real parents? I mean, how do we do this so it doesn't sound suspicious or crazy?"

"I'm not sure. I haven't thought much about anything else while dealing with Mary. But you're right, we need to make sure she understands this is for real."

"What about this? I'll open the call and tell her I've found you and have ended my quest and then tell her you'd like to say 'Hi' to the girl you've heard so much about. That would be a credible way to start the conversation. Then I'll hand you the phone and you begin by saying a simple 'hello' to her and then tell her you have something important to say. Then you tell her she's talking to her birth mother, and her quest is over too."

"I like it, but I'm scared. I'll have to tell her everything: about giving birth to a baby girl in Salina I wanted named Suze, and abandoning her in the adoption, and then leaving for California. Tom, I don't know if I can do it; it's tearing me apart. I'm ashamed to tell her I'm the person who gave her up and ran out—leaving her to strangers. How do I say I've been thinking about her all these years, hoping the best for her, but had no way of finding any information? Will she understand it wasn't allowed, or will she think it's just a shitty, lame excuse? What is she going to think of me?"

"Dianne, she left home to look for you. What do you think that means? It doesn't mean she hates you and doesn't want to see you. Believe me; it's going to be all right."

"I hope so, but I feel so guilty. What kind of mother will she think I'd have been? Now I'm wondering if we should even do this."

"Don't try to have that discussion with yourself. You'll never resolve it alone; it has to be with her. Just know that it's likely to come up at some point, but it probably won't be right away. She's too intrigued with the mystery of finding you and who you are to want to be confrontational. I never detected the slightest trace of bad feelings in her voice when she talked about you. She's longing to find out who you are. It'll be okay, trust me."

"Thanks for that, I do trust you about her. But is she going to believe us—with this fantastic story?"

"Look, it's probable she'll remember she told me the story about how she got her name and might think I told it to you. So it's only logical that she'll be wondering about it. We have to have a way to avoid this looking like some kind of put-on."

"Yes, that's true. I don't want her to start doubting us and that it's a trap. From what you've told me about the days you spent together, she probably trusts you, but that'll only be up to some point. You really have to be considered a stranger, despite the time you spent together on the trip."

"Okay, so here's what we do. She never told me her birthdate, so you couldn't have learned it from me if I didn't know it. But you know that, and where and when she was born down to the hospital, hour and minute. Just tell her that!"

"Yes! That's perfect. There's no reason you would know that about her, and I'm probably the only person in the world, except maybe her adoptive mother, who knows those facts. Her aunt Julie probably doesn't even know the details. Okay, I think I can do it. Let's call now, please."

After several rings, the answering machine gave the usual, "Hi, we're not available now, please leave a message and we'll get back to you."

I left another message giving my name and reminding them that I was the guy who'd delivered Suze to their home the previous week. "I have an important message for Suze and I'd appreciate a callback as soon as possible." I left Dianne's house phone number, as well as my car phone's number again, with the preference they call Dianne's house phone first.

While we waited, hoping for a quick callback, we spoke about the darker side of the adoption process. "How did you handle the adoption agency's questions about Suze's father and the inquiries they do to seek the father's permission for an adoption?"

"I told them it was rape and that I had no idea who the father might be, and furthermore that I wouldn't want him involved in it even if I could name him. Of course, they wanted more. Did I file a complaint with the police? Did I inform my parents or any friends? Why was I wanting to do this in Kansas instead of Ohio? A whole list of questions that were intrusive and embarrassing. Many of my answers were lies. I hated it all . . . and it made me feel cheap and miserable. Not only was I lying to everyone, including my aunt and uncle, but I had the embarrassment of sitting in front of strangers who were asking questions about very intimate things. I sat on a hard, folding chair in a room with two women: an unmarried pregnant girl being grilled like a prisoner. I felt like a pariah, and I knew they didn't believe me." On the verge of tears, Dianne hesitated, looking for a way to continue her story.

I stopped her and tried to tell her I would have done anything—including marrying her, "My God, Dianne, I'm so sorry you went through that. It's a useless thing to say at this point, but—"

"Then don't say it. It doesn't help, and it's all over now, anyway. Let's forget those months and move on. And don't ask me to forgive you because there is nothing to forgive. You didn't do anything wrong. It just happened and I'm happy you're here now."

"I—"

"Don't. Let's talk to Suze and we'll go from there."

"Dianne, I'm sorry to ask these questions, but I want to understand what you went through. How were your aunt and uncle with this? Did they help you? What did they want you to do?"

"Well, in 1968 you didn't mention the word 'abortion' in Harold's house, or anywhere in Kansas for that matter. I had the psychological bruises to prove it. It was 'have the baby or get out of my house.' I didn't have any options, so I stayed there and had Suze. And then I got out of his house. It was the worst time of my life."

"From the conversation I had with your dad a few months ago, when I was still back in Dayton, and what you just told me about your attempt to see him, I can't imagine you'd have considered going back to live with him to have the baby?"

"Hell no! He hated me. One night, a few weeks before I left, he told me he didn't want me ever coming to his house again. It was after we'd had the usual arguments about the war and politics and religion—all that bullshit. He hated everything about Antioch and what the people there stood for. He told me to get the hell to California where I could live with all the hippies and drug addicts. That's where I belonged! And you know what? He was right about me belonging out here!"

"You know he probably has Alzheimer's, or at least severe dementia now."

"I know. I call him every few weeks, but it's useless. He doesn't know who I am and he doesn't remember anything . . . even from the last time I called."

"Dianne—"

She placed a finger across my lips, saying, "No, Tom; there's no need to talk of this anymore. The VA is going to take care of him, I made sure of that. People who write magazine articles and books, and have been reporters with the *LA Times* can figure out who to talk to—and do carry some weight."

She kissed me on the lips: a long, warm—not hot and passionate—kiss. It seemed the perfect thing for the circumstances.

The Call

There was no return call from San Diego the rest of that evening, nor the next morning.

We'd decided to drive down to Monterey for a late breakfast and walk through the shops around Cannery Row. After starting the Jeep and heading for Moss Landing where we'd turn and connect with Highway 101, I noticed the car phone's display indicating there were messages waiting on my voice-recording service. Because I didn't use it often, the car phone was more of an afterthought and I wasn't in the habit of bringing it in with me every night. It was a car phone, so messages might wait until the next time I used the car. I dialed the message service number.

A stuttering voice said, "Hi Mr. Patter . . . Hi Tom, it's Suze. I'm . . . I'm in a little bit of trouble here in San Diego. Would you call me back as soon as possible please? I'm wait . . . waiting by the public phones in a hotel by the freeway close to where my aunt and uncle live." She left the number of the pay phone in a teary, tight-sounding voice. The call had been made at 11:05 pm the previous evening.

And there was another message, left an hour and a half after the first one. I turned the volume up so we both could hear. Her voice now sounded tense and in a higher pitch than the first call.

"Hi Tom, it's Suze again. I know it's late, but please call when you get this. I've been here in the lobby for hours with the hotel people watching me and I'm worried they're going to make me leave. I want to tell you that I packed my suitcase and left Aunt Julie's house a few hours ago. I'd like to talk to you about it, but if we don't connect tonight, I'll keep trying tomorrow. I have no idea of where I'll be then, so it probably won't do any good to call this number in the morning. I don't know what to do, and I'm a little worried, so that's why I'm calling you. When I get to a safe place . . . I . . . I'll call again." Her voice faded into a squeaky, even higher pitch.

"Jesus Christ, it was Suze! She's in trouble. Those calls were both made late last night from a pay phone in a hotel in San Diego! She packed up her clothes and left her aunt's house."

"Oh, fuck! Tom, call the number to see if anyone answers."

I pulled over to the side of the road and dialed the hotel pay phone number, but as I expected, there was no answer. "Dianne, I think we should cancel this trip and go back to your place to see if anyone at the aunt's house in San Diego has called back yet. If not, I'm going to call there again. I'm really worried."

"I am too. That poor girl is out wandering around in places she isn't familiar with and doesn't have any friends out here. This makes me sick!"

There were no new calls on Dianne's house phone voice recorder. I called Aunt Julie's home phone again but there was still no answer. I left another message to call Dianne's phone number, explaining that was where I was staying and would be at that number for the next few days. I also left the car phone number again.

"Now what?" I asked, mostly to myself.

"Call that pay phone again. Let it ring until someone answers it. When someone does, ask for the hotel manager or someone at the front desk. You can ask if anyone knows anything about a girl waiting by that phone last night."

"Might as well, maybe someone will answer it if I keep calling."

The phone rang and rang until an automated phone system message came on the line telling me there was no answer and to try later. I was then cut off. I waited five minutes and called again with the same results. I waited a few more minutes and tried again. Finally, someone picked up the phone and irritably asked who was calling and if I knew this was a pay phone in the lobby of the Western Hotel. The person answering was the day shift front desk agent. I explained why I was calling and told him it was urgent that I talk to anyone who'd seen a girl calling from that phone last night and had been waiting for a return call. He said he hadn't been on duty then but would try to find out if anyone on shift had heard anything about it. I gave him Dianne's house phone number and he promised to call back within a few minutes.

We drank tea and watched the surf while waiting for the callback, which finally came more than an hour later. The hotel manager said he'd talked to the night manager who told him there had been a girl sitting through the evening in a chair by the lobby phones, and that he finally had to tell her he didn't have any vacancies and couldn't offer her a room. He'd offered to call a few nearby hotels to check on vacancies for her, but she declined, saying she needed to be moving on. He finally advised her that she wouldn't be allowed to stay in the lobby overnight and she'd need to leave. She hadn't argued about it, and he helped her get her suitcase out the front doors sometime after 1:00 am. He watched as she walked, dragging that huge bag to the all-night Denny's restaurant next door. After that, he'd returned to his desk and forgot about the incident.

"That's all I can tell you, Mr. Patterson. I wish I could be of more help, but that's the story."

"I understand, thank you."

"Jesus Christ, Dianne; our daughter just walked out into the night at 1:00 am in a town where she's a stranger with no place to go. Imagining her dragging that suitcase across a dark parking lot to an all-night Denny's is horrifying. I want to throw up."

"I'm already crying." She wiped tears from her eyes. "Tom, please call that Denny's and ask if anyone knows what happened to her."

After checking with the daytime staff, Denny's day-shift manager didn't have any information about a young girl with a suitcase coming into the restaurant at 1:00 am that morning. We'd need to wait until the night-shift staff came back at 9:00 pm and call then. He said he'd leave a note advising the night shift manager we'd be calling about her. I protested that I didn't want to lose the entire day, and this couldn't wait that long. I asked for the night-shift manager's home phone number. He said it was against company policy to give out employee's personal information. He offered to try reaching him at home and would get back to us if he had anything.

"Call the San Diego police and see if they've had any reports about a young girl going missing," Dianne asked me.

The San Diego Police Department refused to take a missing person's report because I couldn't claim that Suze was truly missing. That was compounded by the fact that neither Dianne nor I had legal standing since we weren't relatives-of-record. I didn't want to go into the whole "We're-her-real-parents" and adoption story at that point, so I was just a person reporting a mysterious phone call as far as they were concerned. They weren't going to put out a missing person report only on my worries, and they needed confirmation by someone else. But they promised to send an officer to do more checking on the story at both the Western Hotel and Denny's located on Mira Mesa Boulevard, near the freeway. I gave the officer Julie's and Mike's names, phone number, and home address, explaining they could get confirmation from them. He agreed they'd talk to Julie and Mike to verify my story.

"We can't sit around here, waiting until nine o'clock tonight to talk to the Denny's night manager, or for the San Diego police to call back at who-knows-when," Dianne said, exasperation showing all over her face. "Can't we do more?"

"The only thing I can think of is calling the Denny's manager again, tell him this situation is turning into an emergency, and ask him if he's found anything about Suze. And I'll lean on him again to give us the home phone number of that night manager. Or maybe I can ask him to have the night manager call here."

⁓

"Hi, I'm Todd White. Our day-shift manager told me you're looking for information on a customer we had in the restaurant last night. What can I do for you?"

I told him I was hoping someone working last night might have seen and talked to a girl walking alone, pulling a large blue suitcase into his restaurant.

"What's your relation to her? Why should I tell you about her?"

I gave him the entire story about being her original birth father, that I'd dropped her off with her adoption aunt and uncle near the restaurant, and my conversation with the hotel night manager. And I told him about the phone call she'd left for me.

"Look, I don't want to get into the middle of a fight between people claiming to be someone's original parents playing tug-of-war with the adopting parents. I did talk to some people last night who said they were the aunt and uncle of a runaway girl. They had questions about her. They couldn't prove they had any relationship with her either: no photo's or details on what she might be wearing, so I was suspicious of them. They seemed more angry than worried. Look, you should go to the police with this and sort it out with them."

"Were their names Julie and Mike?"

"Yes, that sounds right. They came in about an hour after she'd left. By the way, what was the girl's name?"

"Suze." I spelled it out for him: "S-U-Z-E."

"I didn't know the spelling, just that they called her Susie, or I guess, Suze," he said emphasizing the Z. You really need to talk to the police."

"I already have, and I'm waiting for them to send someone over to the hotel and your restaurant. They said they would go to the aunt and uncle's place, too. Look, this is on the level. I'm doing this the right way and am not trying to do something sneaky or dishonest. And, by the way, she's twenty-two, so she's responsible for herself. Can't you tell me any more?"

"Okay, I'll take your word for it. I'll tell you the same thing I told the other two. She sat alone in a booth for a while with a soft drink, looking out the windows into the parking lot. She looked kinda teary to me, like she was fighting off crying. Her face was flushed, and she used a napkin to wipe her nose and eyes a lot."

"What happened to her? Do you have any idea?"

My heart sank when he said, "She left with a group of guys who were in a rock band."

"Is that it? Can't you tell me anymore?"

"A little. There weren't any other customers in the restaurant, so I was watching them all. They were practicing songs and weren't too bad, but the guy trying to sing the high part wasn't getting it. They were singing 'Take it to the Limit'—you know the Eagles' song? But after going through it a couple of times, they tried it without any falsetto voice and that wasn't working either. They were going through it another time when your girl, Suze, sitting a couple of booths away, comes in on the high part and just absolutely nailed it."

"That sounds like Suze."

"Those guys were knocked out! One of them, probably their front singer, went over and started talking to her. Pretty soon he sat down in her booth and they were laughing and talking away when the rest of them, four more guys, went over to her booth too. One of them had a guitar and started playing chords and she started singing, 'In the Long Run,' solo. And she was just nailing that too."

I listened as he went on, "They didn't finish the song; they stopped half way through and started talking about a gig they were going to up at Tahoe. I couldn't hear everything, but it sounded like they were trying to get her to go with them and sing with the band. That's about it. They paid their own, and her bills, got her suitcase and left. They all got into a big white SUV; probably a Suburban, pulling a small trailer, and drove away."

"Tahoe! Did you hear them mention any clubs they'd be playing? Did you get the name of the band or any of the members?"

"No, none of that. They were all talking so fast and all over each other, I could only pick up little pieces of it."

"Damn! I wish you had heard just one name to give me something to start with."

"Sorry. But if it means anything, all the songs they seemed to be working with were Eagles songs. So maybe they're an Eagles cover band. But I did hear her mention Linda Ronstadt once. Maybe they do her music too."

"Can you give me the name on the credit card used to pay the bill?"

"Sorry, I couldn't do that, but they paid cash anyway. The guy that paid had a pretty big roll of bills he peeled some twenties from."

"I don't know if I should feel good about that or not. It might mean they're a clean bunch of musicians—or it might mean they're into dealing drugs."

"Well, they looked pretty much okay to me. I mean they didn't look or act like they were druggies or bangers. They actually were pretty well dressed—for musicians, if you know what I mean."

"Well, that's good to hear. Thanks very much for all this, Todd. By the way, how long does it take to drive from there to Tahoe if you don't stop for anything more than gas or a quick stop at a fast food place?"

"I haven't done it for years, but probably ten or eleven hours."

"If they left your place at what, 2:00 am, they'd be there around noon or 1:00 pm today?"

"Probably. That's what I'd figure it taking."

"Okay. Did you tell the aunt and uncle all of this too?"

"Most of it. I don't think I told them all the details of how they met up and of her singing, though. For some reason, I didn't think they'd be interested. They weren't the friendliest people."

I thanked him and hung up.

I'd been using the speakerphone so Dianne could listen. Her mind raced far ahead of mine, and it was clear to me why Tim, at the *Times,* had said she was a great reporter. "Tom, we should call the San Diego police and ask them to contact the Tahoe Police. Maybe we can get them on the lookout for the band and Suze."

"Yes, thank you officer. I know you can't tell Tahoe she's a missing person. But can't you tell them she said she was in trouble? Do I need to connect you to my answering service so you can hear her for yourself?"

I listened as the officer told me I didn't need to do that, but to not erase the message in case they might need it later. He said he would take my word for it and contact Tahoe. He also told me they'd tried to contact Julie and Mike by phone, but there was no answer.

I slid off the kitchen bar stool I'd been sitting on during the phone call. "Dianne, let's go to Tahoe. Grab some clothes and we'll leave in half an hour."

She swung around on her stool to look at me, questions on her face, "Okay, what's the plan? What will we do there?"

"More than we can do here. We're going to turn over every stone looking for five guys in a rock band, with one girl singer, and a white Suburban."

"But I don't want to miss any calls that might come here."

"You have a remote listening code for your answering machine, right?"

"Yes."

"And I have my car phone. What more do we need?"

"You're right. We can do more there than sitting by the telephone here, waiting for a call. Let's go."

"What's the best way to go? Do you have a map?"

"I have all kinds from my trips to concerts all over the state. I've done several up at Tahoe." She walked over to the kitchen alcove, opened a cabinet door above her computer desk, and sorted through a handful of folded highway maps. "Here it is."

"Did you drive to those, or fly?"

"Both, depending on how much time I had, and the weather. It's usually faster to drive since there aren't any direct connections from Monterey to Tahoe. There are a few from San Jose, but it's a pain in the ass to drive over there, take the flight, and then get a car to use there. I found I might as well drive and enjoy the trip. That is if the weather's good and it's not snowing in the mountains."

"Let's check the weather. Do you know where to call?"

Telephone in hand, she replied, "I'm already dialing! Believe me, I keep all the regional weather forecast numbers handy in my little black book."

—◠—

"They're saying Rt. 50, usually the best way to drive from here, is going to be closing by late afternoon because of a storm system bringing in snow at anything over six thousand feet. Rt. 120 is the next route to the south that goes all the way through the Sierras and will get the storm later. It has a 70 percent chance of rain in the afternoon or early evening, changing to light to moderate snow above eight thousand feet. The western entrance to Tioga pass will probably be closed by five or six pm. Just so you know, the elevation at Tioga Pass summit is a little under ten thousand feet, so there definitely is going to be snow up there."

"Can we get over the mountains before they close the highway?"

"Maybe. It's nearly noon now, so we'll still be up in the Tuolumne Meadows area in late afternoon. It'll be close; we won't be over Tioga Pass until at least six pm, but we should be able to make it before the weather gets too bad. You're a winter weather driver from Ohio and have a four-wheel drive Jeep; let's try it."

"Yes, but western Ohio is billiard-table flat. But I have all-weather tires; fuck it, let's go."

"We need to go now then, to try to miss that bad weather that's moving in up there. Let's pack."

"I'm still mostly packed; won't take me more than five minutes."

In the bedroom, as Dianne threw some jeans and shirts into a suitcase, she looked over at me as I was doing the same. "This whole thing is incredible, Tom: you show up a few days ago, tell me you've driven our daughter across country, Mary dies and we had a memorial for her yesterday. And now we're doing a mad dash over the Sierras today to look for Suze! More has happened to us in the last few days than in the last twenty-two years."

"Yeah, can you believe it? It's crazy! Like things have been building up behind a locked door that was just opened."

"Except for losing Mary, I love all of it. And Mary was going to die anyway, whether you found me or not. I guess it's good to have something pulling me out of that darkness, but bittersweet doesn't begin to describe it."

I kissed her, "I know." I changed the topic. "So, we go north, around Yosemite on 120, over Tioga Pass and down to Lee Vining? And then roughly another hundred miles north to South Tahoe? Sounds like around six to eight hours depending on the weather?"

"Yes. There is an alternative by going south to Tehachapi Pass, which is much lower and might not even get the storm, but that would add six or eight hours to the trip. Trust me, I don't think we should do that."

"I've always trusted you. I still do."

"I remember that about you," she said, pulling me into a tight embrace. "Let's go find our daughter."

But I believe in love, I believe in music
I believe in magic, and I believe in you

Tioga Pass

We made slow progress after turning on route 120 where the road forks, with one direction leading sightseers into the heart of Yosemite Valley and the other over Tioga Pass. We weren't sightseers; our mission was taking us up into the high Sierras and then down into Owens Valley at Lee Vining. Fortunately, traffic was sparse, probably due to news of the approaching storm, and it thinned out even more the higher our road climbed. We hit light rain above five thousand feet, with visibility declining as we moved higher into the cloud layers with the result that we were driving in both cloud-fog and rain. Even with the light traffic, most of which moved very slowly under the bad driving conditions, passing straggling vehicles was risky. But our choices were either poking along behind slow drivers into ever-worsening conditions or passing the slow cars and trucks, aiming to get over the mountains faster. We opted for trying to shorten the time we were at high altitude in marginal and degrading driving conditions.

The rain turned into sleet as we moved above seven thousand feet, resulting in a slippery road surface and an icy windshield that had become difficult for the wipers to keep free of ice build-up. I blasted the inside of the windshield with hot defroster air, with fans turned up to the highest setting, to help the wipers by heating the glass from the inside, but they still were barely coping.

Sleet turned into light snow at eight thousand feet and then moderate to heavy snow at the ninety-nine-hundred-foot summit. The highway center line was invisible beneath several inches of snow at summit altitude, and there were now no vehicle tracks to follow. The road edges were also invisible, leaving me no alternative other than just trying to stay in the center of the white space between the trees and boulders lining the roadway. We were alone, on a highway at nearly ten thousand feet, with bad weather closing in on us, driving in a tunnel of snow and fog, with nearly forty miles yet to go.

Dianne was calm and reassuring, encouraging me with gentle suggestions and comments about us nearing the worst of it and soon to start descending out of the bad weather to drier roads.

"We don't have to meet a schedule, Tom. If we get there an hour or two later, it's not going to make any difference. You're doing a great job. Stay cool."

"I agree; we can get there when we get there. My bladder doesn't want to hear that, but my brain says, 'Listen to her, she's always been the smartest person you've ever known.'"

"Yes, brain over bladder. Like sitting through a bad pop concert so I didn't miss something needing to be ripped up. But in recent years, I took the bladder over brain option because most of it was bad and I wouldn't have to listen to it all."

"Why would you put yourself through that? Couldn't they get someone else?"

"Do that too many times and they don't call anymore. And I want to at least stay current on what's happening in music."

"I think, if I had your ability, I'd concentrate on anything but current pop music."

"Then I'd be walking away from more than half of my income. I'm not able to do that, yet."

"We have to do something about that—"

"We? How?"

"What Mary asked me?"

"Stay? I think I mentioned something about that, too, didn't I? But, let's concentrate on driving through this bad weather. If we find Suze, there's a new dimension to that. We can talk about it after."

Highway 120 is relatively level for several miles once up at the summit altitude of Tioga Pass. The curves are gentle with no hairpin turns and only modest elevation changes. But great care needed to be taken with steering and braking up there in those conditions. The Jeep wanted to fishtail and snake scarily around when anything more than easy-does-it pedal pressure was applied. The only way to handle the conditions was by keeping our speed low, at around twenty to twenty-five miles per hour, and avoiding abrupt changes in throttle position, braking and steering. I was driving on eggshells.

Finally, a still legible highway sign not covered with sleet and snow, with squiggly lines painted on it, appeared, warning of a steep, long, curvy grade ahead: TEN MILES. TRUCKS USE LOW GEAR, STAY IN RIGHT LANE.

The grade down to Lee Vining.

I maintained my cautious driving regimen and finally, dropping below the summit, the visibility began to improve slightly as we slipped out of the densest cloud layers. But a frightening view lay ahead. As far as we could see, the downhill grade was covered with a layer of undisturbed, trackless snow.

"Oh shit, look at that," escaped from my mouth.

Dianne reached over and touched my arm, "You're doing fine, Tom, just stay with it." She gave me a brave, encouraging smile. "You can do it."

I remembered what it was like to have the trust and encouragement of a woman. Dylan supplied the words, again:

If not for you, Babe, I couldn't find the door, couldn't even see the floor. It had been too long.

We carefully descended the long grade, keeping our speed down to fifteen miles per hour through curves, with a low block wall—only half the height of the Jeep's wheels—between the roadway and drop-offs of hundreds, or in a few places thousands, of feet off to the passenger side. Some straightaways didn't even have the low block walls. Eternity grinned and beckoned us from the road's edge.

The driving challenge was one of balancing between engine braking and the wheel brakes. For a nerve-wracking ten miles, I sat on the edge of my seat with death grips, one on the steering wheel, and the other on the shift lever, my foot resting gently on the brake pedal. There were times when I didn't get it right and the Jeep, even with its marvelous four-wheel drive, slid frighteningly until we slowed enough to get things back under control. And then it was more of the same: mile after mile, the rocky mountain side looming over us out my window, and the abyss waiting out Dianne's. Half way down that long grade, the desert-like Owens Valley and ghostly Mono Lake appeared and disappeared through light, hazy cloud layers in fading twilight, more than two thousand feet below us. I silently prayed, *please God, just let us get out of the clouds and down to dry roads!*

Several turns and hundreds of feet farther down the grade we found state troopers from the California Highway Patrol stopping uphill traffic at a barricade erected across the road. They were turning vehicles without four-wheel drive around and sending them back down the mountain. Those with four-wheel drive had to put on tire chains before going on up the mountain. No tire chains meant going back down to dry roads. With disbelief in his eyes, a trooper stopped us, "Where the hell have you been? Did you come across the pass?"

"Yes sir," I answered, feeling guilty and stupid, and that I should be apologizing for something. But I also felt a little heroic for having made it.

"They were supposed to be stopping everything at five pm. How did you get through?"

"I guess I was the last one. I didn't see any headlights behind me all the way here. It was pretty lonely up there."

"You're lucky you didn't have an accident. No one would have found you until the snowplows cleared the roads. Coulda' been two or three days."

"I guess so. Can I go now? We've still got to get to Tahoe yet tonight."

"Consider yourselves very lucky. Be careful on that last stretch up to Tahoe. It's snowing on the 50 if you're going into South Tahoe."

"Yes, sir. And thanks for the advice." We drove on.

"What do you think, Dianne? We've still got to deal with Highway 50. Can we get up there?"

"I believe we can. The east part of 50 is on the downslope coming over the Sierras. It's a major access road into and out of South Tahoe. My guess is they'll have had the plows out working it to keep it clear. Gotta' get those gamblers up to the tables . . . ."

"Okay then, Lee Vining coming up and then on to Tahoe. We'll stop in Lee Vining for gas and a sandwich too, if you'd like."

"Sounds good to me. That was a scary ride, but I'm enjoying this, Tom. Even under these circumstances, I love being with you again. It makes me remember drives we used to take around Ohio and that trip we took together to Indiana. It was so much fun until I went and ruined everything."

"It hurt a lot, Dianne. But you were just doing what was in your heart. I understood it was something you had to do."

"And you did what you had to do, too."

"Yeah, I guess I did . . . ." I was feeling torn between memories of Sara and the excitement I felt about being here with Dianne. *Should I be feeling this way, enjoying myself with my old girlfriend like this? I can't help it, I can't stop myself. . . .*

The rest of the road down to Lee Vining was dry and smooth. We were treated to the spectacular eastern view out over Owens Valley and strange Mono Lake with the Nevada desert beyond, in long, grey-blue shadows cast by the weak remaining sunlight reflecting through and under the clouds over the Sierras.

I had a guilty feeling, but said it anyway. "I know it's my fault; we could have been doing things like this together for the last twenty years."

She looked at me with a sad smile, but an agreeing look in her eyes, "Yes but we're doing it now . . . ."

"We created a baby after that Indiana trip who we've never known for twenty-two years. Let's find her and give her a home—if she'll have us. What do you think?" I asked.

"You mean, like a mom and dad? What are you saying, Tom?"

"Well . . . ."

My mouth had been ahead of my brain. I didn't have a ready answer to her question and was glad she took me off the hook by cutting me off saying, "Don't answer that. We can talk about it after we find her. Jesus, I hope we can find her before something happens. I wonder if her aunt and uncle are looking for her in Tahoe too."

"They might be. Truthfully, they should be. I don't think they'd want to tell Suze's Kansas parents that she ran away from them, too. They wouldn't be happy to hear that."

"Yes, it makes me wonder what happened in San Diego. And then there's that rock band; five guys and just Suze."

"A rock and a hard place . . . ." Dianne said, staring at the view unfolding through the windshield.

Revelations

As we approached the intersection with US 395 south of Lee Vining, the Jeep's car phone started flashing its message waiting light.

"Get that, will you? The access code is 111."

"Well, that's tricky." She picked up the receiver and held it above the center console so we could both listen.

"Hi Mr. Patterson, it's Suze again." We looked at each other in astonishment.

"I wish I could talk to you instead of leaving messages all the time, but I guess you're out of connection range or something. I hope you received the other messages I left for you last night—it was actually early this morning—so you'll know what's happened. It's noon, twelve-fifteen on Friday and I'm in a Chevron gas and fast food store in a place called Lee Vining."

We stared at each other with mouths wide open as she continued in rapid fire, girl-in-a-hurry monologue. "I'm on my way to Lake Tahoe with a band I met after I left that hotel in San Diego. Don't be alarmed when you hear this; they seem like pretty good guys and they needed a back-up singer. They asked me to come along to Tahoe for a one-week gig they have at a place called Whiskey Creek. I have no idea what the place is like, but they said it was a small western style, dining-music club with good clientele and pay. The name of the band is The Falcons and we do Eagles and other '70s country rock. I'm hoping to get them to do a little Ronstadt, too. We've been practicing my parts on the drive up here. Look, I have to go now, they're all standing around by the gas pumps looking for me. I want to tell you about why I left Aunt Julie's house when we can talk longer. Mike was out of control, and I couldn't trust him when Julie wasn't home. But I'll wait to tell you more later. Don't worry about me, the band members are all married or in long-term relationships except for the drummer, Jimmy. I think I'm okay with them. Some of the girls are coming up for the weekend to see their guys perform, so I think it's going to be fun and I'll have some companionship. Jimmy's a little strange though, but I think he's okay. Look, I've gotta' go—"

Another voice could be heard in the background, "C'mon, c'mon, dammit, don't . . . ."

We heard her say, sounding like she was at a short distance from the phone, "Wait, Jimmy! Mr. Patterson, please try to call me at Whiskey—" The line went dead.

"Oh fuck, Tom! Jesus Christ, did someone grab her?"

"I don't know, I heard it too. That was seven hours ago, they must be in Tahoe by now. Let's get there!"

We turned north on Highway 395, and as we were driving out of town through the northern side of Lee Vining looking for a gas and convenience store, we spotted the Chevron station and pulled into the gas pump area.

"I'll gas the car up, Dianne, and you can go in to see if anyone working in there remembers seeing her. I'll join you as soon as it's full to help with her description if they need it."

<hr />

Dianne was standing at the checkout counter, talking to the clerk on the opposite side by the cash register. "She says she remembers a young girl in the phone booth by the restrooms around noon making a call," Dianne said to me as I walked to the checkout counter. "Her friends were out in the pump driveway looking around for her when one of the guys came in to get her. She was trying to finish her call, and he was motioning at her and saying, 'Come on, don't be a pain in the ass.' She held up a finger, like 'one minute,' when he grabbed her by the arm and just pulled her away from the phone and left it hanging there."

"How was she acting? I mean, was she angry or scared looking?" Dianne asked.

"Well . . . it was more like she was half laughing and half mad. She didn't scream or anything, but she was resisting him a little. Finally, she gave in and jogged along to a white Suburban with him. That's about it. I can't tell you what it meant," said the counter clerk.

⌒→

"Okay, we know the place they'll be playing, we know the name of the band, and we now know for sure it's a white Suburban," I said after we'd cleared the little roadside business establishments and had open highway ahead.

"Why don't we use the car phone and call the Tahoe Police now to give them an update?" Dianne asked me.

"Good idea. Will you do it, please?"

The Tahoe Police dispatch officer who answered the phone didn't seem to be aware of the situation with Suze. It wasn't clear if they'd ever received the call from San Diego, or if someone who took the call hadn't alerted the rest of the office.

"She said they'd be on the lookout for a white Suburban towing a trailer, but since we couldn't give them a plate number and there's always a fleet of white Suburban's in Tahoe, they'd be lucky to stumble onto it. And she said she's never been to Whiskey Creek but knows it's out on Highway 89 somewhere."

"I know what to do; I'll give twenty bucks to the head bellman wherever we end up staying for the night and ask him to get the details on Whiskey Creek. He gets another twenty when he brings back information. When in doubt, ask a bellman; those guys either know everything, or know how to get the stuff they don't know."

"And if that doesn't work, we could talk to any local bands playing in the hotels or clubs on the Tahoe strip and ask them."

"That's good! We can try that if we need. You do know how to do this kind of thing, don't you?"

"What do you think I learned being a reporter in LA for six years? It's about more than just writing the story. You have to get it first!"

⌣⟶

The storm was dropping out of the Sierras into the Owens valley with light rain falling on the highway. We still had two more hours of careful driving in front of us.

"How are you feeling about Mary?" I asked after driving in silence for fifteen minutes with the soft, mesmerizing clicking of the windshield wipers nearly hypnotizing me. After the long drive through and over the Sierras, I needed conversation to stave off drowsiness.

"I'm okay; dealing with it, I guess. It was such a long, drawn-out illness—around six months—that I knew it was coming and tried to get ready mentally for it in the last several weeks. But then it's always harder than you think it's going to be. The poor girl, she had a rough time of it ever since Pete's death."

"That's more than ten years."

"Yes, she loved that first job she had with the real estate development company, but it wasn't enough. After Pete died, she could barely force herself to go to work. The company tried to be good to her and gave her several weeks off, but she never really got her head back into it. That's probably what made her vulnerable when the real estate market crashed a year later and her company had to cut expenses. Even though she'd been awarded all kinds of bonuses in previous years, she was one of the first to go. And that was after I'd left the *Times* and had started out on my own. We didn't have enough money and were living hand to mouth."

"And that led to the Jim Carver affair?"

"Yes, the bastard. But I've already told you about most of that, except for when Mary tried to kill herself a little while later."

"Mary mentioned that she'd tried to commit suicide in that last conversation I had with her before she died. Pete's death caused it?"

"She was still depressed from losing Pete. And then the Carver thing happened about a year later. We both thought hanging out with Carver for some good times would help her get over Pete's death. But I think it only made it worse; the more fun we tried to have, the guiltier she seemed to feel for trying to have fun. The next year, long after the episode when I hit him with the frying pan, she tried dating a couple of other guys who didn't work out, and she blamed herself. I think she believed her life was over, so why drag it out. Why not just end it? I came home from an interview and found her unconscious in bed with an empty sleeping pill bottle."

"How did you save her?"

"I called 911; they were there in a flash and saved her. God bless those guys and girls!"

"She told me she tried suicide again."

"One time I came home from a . . . a . . . little time I'd taken away. . . . Oh hell, Tom, I'll tell you. I was living on and off with a guy I liked very much. I liked him enough that I thought I could marry him. He was a musician—a very good musician who mostly did recording studio work. He played guitar and keyboards and was in demand all the time around the LA music scene. He's played with a lot of big names who wanted something special on their recordings."

"Would I know his name?"

"Probably not, unless you read all the fine print about who played which instruments on which song in the album notes. Most people never see that information and can't be bothered with it. People don't realize that the musicians they see on stage in some big-name road trips aren't the same musicians who helped make the hits in the first place. There are a lot of expert musicians who don't like touring and prefer staying in the studio, making really first-class recordings."

"Yeah, I know that. Some artists don't even have full time bands and just get the best studio musicians they can when they go into the recording studio. That was the case with Dylan too. He had different musicians for New York who were different from the Nashville people or the LA people. Same thing with Steely Dan now."

"So, you understand then. Well, Dave was one of the studio types who never toured. Never . . . except after I started going with him . . . unfortunately."

"What happened?"

"I was living with him when he got a call from a producer who was putting together a big tour with some of the best groups at that time. He liked it because he'd be able to play in multiple performances with the different artists, which appealed to him and was the main reason he wanted to do it. But the money was very good, so he accepted the offer and did the tour. I went back to the apartment Mary and I had been sharing for the four months he was on tour. Mary was glad to have me back, but I could tell she wasn't happy that I'd been gone for several weeks at the time."

"What was the problem? Didn't she like the guy?"

"It wasn't that. I could tell she was going into another depression over Pete and needed me around to keep her out of it. She just wasn't able to keep it together when she was alone. But over the four months I was back, she came out of it and things were fine."

"So, then what?"

"I went back to Dave's when he came off the tour. He wasn't the same guy. He'd been on drugs the whole time and was a basket case. He, actually we, smoked a little grass now and then when he was doing the studio work, but that was it. He was very adamant that he'd never get into the hard drugs. But I think being around it all the time with the heavy users on the tour finally got to him; he joined the party. It took me months to get him out of it. I can't tell you how hard it is to be with someone going through that. It's just an ugly mess."

"I'm a little surprised you stayed with him. I can't imagine you putting up with it."

"Well, I wanted him back with me the way it was before, and I have to admit that I had a secondary motive. Being part of the LA music scene gave me access to musicians and the recording and touring world. I was in the studio for some phenomenal recording sessions in those years. I got to know a lot of musicians, quite a lot about the music business on the inside, and I had the access I needed to do the interviews and magazine articles I was publishing.

I guess it was a little bit about being opportunistic, but I loved the guy—and the entire music scene."

"What happened from there?"

"He went on another tour, around a year later. Same kind of deal: lots of top musicians and big shows. They went all over the country and played to sold-out, fifty thousand seat ball parks and sports arenas."

"Did he get back into drugs?"

"Yes. That was partly it. I probably could have done the rescue thing with him again, but it was more than that. The drugs took me to the line, but the girls pushed me over it."

"Girls? You mean, like . . . groupies throwing themselves at the musicians?"

Dianne sighed, "Yes. I'd gone back to his apartment to get it ready for his return—you know—clean it up, get in some food and things. I had a key, of course, so when I let myself in and walked into the kitchen, the phone message-waiting light was blinking like crazy and the display was showing a bunch of messages on the recorder. I started to play them, thinking there might be something important he should know about, or even that he'd left one for me since I told him I'd go there and get the place ready for him."

Dianne hesitated, taking a long breath and time to gather her thoughts before going on.

Continuing, her eyes flashed hatred. "Calls from girls all over the fucking country: 'Hi Dave, it's Tammy. I'm just calling to find out if you're back yet. Call me so I can come out and pick up where we left off . . . if you know what I mean. Bye now.' Or 'Hi Davey, can I come out to California so you can play my keyboard again?' And then there was one from a Rhonda or something: 'Hey sweetie, I'd like to have you do that thing you do with your guitar pick between your teeth again, ha ha ha. Call me; here's my number . . . .'"

"All that stuff you read about with musicians on the road."

"God yes! The calls started me thinking about what he'd probably been doing with his body parts, and I decided right then I didn't need to expose myself to whatever they'd experienced—as a way of putting it."

"So, what did you do?"

"I met the bus at the studio just as we'd planned, but ready to unload on him. But the tour manager met me at the bus door and told me I had a big job on my hands: 'You'll find him on one of the sofas in the back of the bus.' I went back there, totally pissed and loaded for war, when I saw him lying in his own vomit, unconscious. That was enough, I went out and found the tour manager and told him, 'He's not my problem anymore; he's your problem!' That was it. I went back to the apartment and loaded up my things and left. I've never seen him again."

"What happened to him?"

"I guess someone got him cleaned up and sober. I heard he was back in the studio and musicians were asking for him again."

"Did you ever hear from him after that?"

"Yes, I don't need to go into all of that. There were all the usual promises to go straight, never to go on tours again, and he wanted to get married and that would solve it all. Bullshit!"

"Sure it would. Did you really love him, Dianne?"

"I thought I did. When he was straight he was the most decent guy a girl could want: thoughtful, fun, a good lover, and just incredible to listen to playing music. But I could never shut out the thoughts of what I'd heard in those phone recordings . . . and visualizing what some of them were describing. I just wasn't going to live with it, no matter how good he was in other ways. He didn't have enough spine to stay straight when he was away. I found that I didn't love him enough to put up with that."

"I guess that's what Mary was talking about when she told me you'd broken off with a guy to be with her."

"It was partly about her, but I broke off for the reasons I just told you. When I got back to our Santa Monica apartment later the same day, Mary was already in the process of trying to kill herself again. She'd taken a bottle of pills and was lying on the floor in the bedroom, awake but vomiting and breathing it back in. I got her out of it and sat her up in a chair to keep her awake. Paramedics got there just in time again. Christ, I went from one disaster to another near disaster in one day! That was when I realized I'd never be able to leave her alone. But, somehow, after finishing off with Dave, helping

Mary seemed like just the thing I needed: something to work for and change my world at the same time. So that's what happened, and we moved up to Sea Grass several months later and have been there since."

"He must be the other bad experience you mentioned the other day."

"Yes, and drugs were at the bottom of both. That's a part of coming to California I didn't expect, or want to happen. I think it tarnished the dream a little, but this is still where I want to live."

"Did coming up to Sea Grass work for you—both of you?"

"Mary changed after that. It seemed she just couldn't be close enough to me. We'd always been very close, as you know, but after that, she centered her life around mine. She did have a good run in that real estate agency in Santa Monica, but her personal life was shot. She didn't have a life of her own anymore; it became all about what I wanted to do, or where I was going. She wanted to go everywhere with me: all over the state to concerts or interviews. It was like she was my shadow. I loved her, but I didn't want her glued to me like that. And that changed me, too. She felt threatened if I wanted to see any-one for just a dinner or a night out with a guy, and so I couldn't imagine going on a date or away for a weekend to come home and find her in the middle of another suicide—or even already dead."

I'd wanted to know more about her relationship with Mary after Pete's death and after they'd moved to Sea Grass Estates but had been afraid to ask. I was starting to get the picture.

⌒⟶

We were silent for a while as we neared the Nevada border, still on US 395. We grazed the California-Nevada border before turning west and heading up into the eastern face of the Sierras and toward Lake Tahoe on Highway 50.

"I know you're wondering about Mary and me, Tom. It's the elephant-in-the-room kind of thing, right?"

"Yes, I have been. But I don't want to pry into your relationship with her. If you tell me you were just housemates, we can leave it there. I remember you were very close back in our Dayton days: holding hands and an occasional embrace or even a kiss. But I always thought it seemed so natural for you two that it didn't bother me at all, and I didn't care. You don't have to say any more about it."

"No, I want you to know. I want you to understand that we didn't have a physical thing going on between us. I'm not a lesbian and neither was Mary. We both had relationships with men. Obviously, Mary and Pete had a normal, loving sexual relationship, except they didn't want to have children because of Pete's racing. And I had a normal, if you want to call it that, man-woman relationship with Dave. Mary and I always had a very close friendship, but it wasn't sexual."

"Okay—"

She cut me off, saying, "But it did change a little after Pete died, though. After the Carver thing and a few short affairs, and then my relationship with Dave, we both were turned off by the men we'd been meeting and basically backed away from the singles scene around LA. Mary became too unstable to have any kind of relationships with men. For me, after Dave, it had all seemed to be about being groped by men wanting one-night stands with no real love involved. It might have been my fault, or it might have been that I was meeting the wrong men—maybe those were the same thing—but I wasn't getting what I wanted. I couldn't seem to meet anyone with some intelligence and my interests. I was going into my forties by then and wasn't looking for Mr. Studly. And I didn't want to end up pregnant by a man I didn't want to marry, or who didn't want to marry me."

I looked sideways and started to say, "Agai—"

She held up her hand to stop me. "It's not the same. Don't try to make that comparison. I would have married you if we saw our futures a little differently. We had the kind of chemistry I thought would work—but not in Dayton."

"You probably believed you'd be able to find someone for yourself out of the millions of men in LA, I guess?"

"Yes. Who wouldn't believe there'd be someone out of all of them? I almost did with Dave, but that went to hell . . . ."

"You know, it's funny; Suze and I had a similar conversation, although it came up in a different way. We were talking about me letting you go. I told her we need to think twice before walking away from the things and people we love, assuming we can just replace them somewhere, sometime later. I should have known that myself back then. I guess we both should have known that back then."

"That's the problem with being young. We don't hold onto important things since we believe we have the rest of our lives to find whoever and whatever we need—when we already have it. 'Youth is wasted on the young', how true is that?"

"Shaw?"

"Well, I'm impressed that you know he said it! But you did find Sara."

"You're probably the one who told me about Shaw. But Sara wasn't you. She was a wonderful wife and mother, and I loved her very much. But she was very different from you."

"How so?"

"She wasn't the bold, exciting person you were—or still are."

"Are you saying she was a second choice? You can't mean that!"

"I'm not trying to say that. It's just that she was a totally different kind of woman than you are—or as I remember you were. Sara was a salt-of-the-earth, religious, family person with Midwestern values. To me, you were very different; even exotic, with very forward-thinking interests and views."

"Exotic! I never thought of myself that way. But doesn't it seem a little strange? Strange that you could have fallen for two women who were so different?"

"I don't think so. I didn't start out with a list of specifications that needed to be met you know. You have one set of qualities and Sara had a different set. But you both are—were—completely wonderful women."

"Exotic and now wonderful! No one out here ever called me those. Where have you been all these years? But, you sound just like an engineer: evaluating parameters, weighing and adding them up."

"And that's exactly what I was trying to avoid sounding like. I don't have a list comparing the two of you; I was trying to just focus on the total package." *Total package? How stupid!* I hated myself before the words disappeared into the car's background noise. I wanted them back.

"Package! Still sounding like an engineer."

"I'm sorry. I guess I can't help myself; you know I've never been very good at expressing myself. I'm still kind of a klutzy nerd I guess."

"I forgive you. And I have to admit that your naïve innocence was something that I always found attractive, you know. But tell me, did Sara like Dylan?"

"No, couldn't stand him." I was thankful she'd changed the subject—for my benefit. "She thought he sounded like a hick singing through his nose and wondered how anyone could like that voice. I tried to explain that she should be listening to the words—the poetry. But she couldn't get past his voice."

"So how did she compensate for that with you? Did she like The Stones, or The Beatles?"

"Ha, no. You probably won't believe this, but she loved classical and gospel music."

"I can understand that. I've reviewed some very good gospel performers. I love the Staple Singers and the Blind Boys of Alabama. And I love string quartets. Was Sara religious?"

"Very. But she wasn't pushy about it. I think she decided I was okay the way I was and so she didn't want to pester me about it. But she had control of the kids."

"How else?"

"Unconditional love."

"I'm not sure I know what that is . . . not sure I've ever seen it."

"What about Pete and Mary? Wasn't that unconditional love?"

"Yes, maybe you're right. There it was, right beneath my nose and I didn't recognize it, probably because I've never personally experienced it," she said with a sad look.

"Sara and I never argued or yelled at each other. We were open with one another and trusted each other completely. She was a good Christian woman who only wanted a happy, secure home life for our family."

"You must miss her badly."

"I do; there's been a huge hole in my life."

Dianne didn't say anything and stared straight ahead, through the windshield. I doubted that she was really seeing anything and I imagined her thinking: *Is he hoping I'm going to fill that hole?* I threw caution to the winds: "If a person gets lucky, he or she might get a second chance," I said.

Curiosity in her face, she nodded and gave me a long look with a questioning smile and raised eyebrows. But she didn't take the bait, probably waiting to see if I was going to say more. And I was waiting for her to say something. We drove on in another silence.

I thought, *My daughter, Susan, is probably waiting for that call I promised to make. But I don't know what the hell I'd tell her at this point.*

"Tom, I do want to finish my thoughts about Mary and me."

"You already told me; you said you weren't lesbian lovers?"

"Not quite like that. We might have been something close to lesbian lovers, but not in the sexual sense. Not the kind that you probably read about in books or hear when men make jokes about lesbians."

"What does that mean?"

"It means we didn't get into the physical things like the stuff in erotic, alternative-lifestyle novels and porn movies, or men's magazines. Somehow, without talking about it, we both knew that wasn't what either of us wanted. We were looking for love and tenderness from each other. And understanding and a hug or a kiss when one of us needed it. We were careful about touching each other; there's a place beyond that where I think neither of us knew how to go. It would have changed everything and I believe we were both afraid of going there."

"I understand—I think. It seems like crossing a certain line could be a point of no-return. That is, if you wanted that option. It seems like a dangerous point."

"Yes, and we didn't want to cross that line. If we did and it turned out to be a bad experience, there was no going back to our previous lives and relationship. So we stopped at that line."

"I really don't know what to say; I've never been in that situation or anything close to it. How do you feel about it now?"

"I'm glad we handled it like we did. Maybe we missed exploring something that would have been the right thing for us, but I never wanted to take that chance. I think everything takes on new meaning when sex is involved. It can get too complicated and emotional. I had enough of that with a guy named Robert—I'll tell you about him sometime—and Dave. And even though nothing ever happened with Carver, that was over sex too. No, I have no regrets about keeping that out of my life with Mary."

"You haven't had any men friends since you moved up here, then?"

"For me, it didn't exclude seeing men. We'd both tried to find Mr. Right, but we kept failing at it. Mary just gave up on it and started clinging to me. I still wanted to find the right guy but was getting nowhere. But after a while, and knowing Mary's dependence on me, I essentially gave up on it too. And thinking about my Robert affair and what that did to me, I decided I didn't want to possibly put Mary in that same situation. Been there, done that . . . ."

Robert? What affair, what situation? I didn't ask.

"But, it's been a long time . . . how many years?"

"Tom, I'm not counting years any more. I've been happy with my life: living here with Mary, my concert reviews, my novels, and magazine work. I just moved on, thinking it wasn't to be—for me."

"I would have never guessed it. I always thought you were the most desirable girl in Dayton."

"That was Dayton; this is California."

"Dayton, California, what's the difference? A desirable woman is a desirable woman anywhere. Like I said, the guys out here must be nuts."

"What can I say, Tom? It wasn't for lack of trying . . . ."

"Okay, I don't want to know how hard you tried." *Or did I?* Now was as good a time as any to ask about something that had always bothered me.

"You sometimes disappeared for complete weekends back in our Dayton days, and no one knew where you were. I always wondered what that was about. I guessed you had someone else I didn't know of and spent those weekends with him, whoever he was. It killed me, thinking you were off with some guy, on a weekend fling."

"Oh, Tom. Do you want to know all my secrets? What'll we have to talk about next week?"

"I'm sorry; you don't have to tell me. It just seemed like the conversation was begging the question. Forget it."

"What the hell, I guess I'm going into all my personal history—all in one long drive. But why not? I'll tell you about it. I think I owe it to you since you were a close part of my life back then and had to wonder what was going on. And—I owe you for coming out to find me."

"But, you don't have to—"

"It wasn't quite what you were thinking . . . close, but not that. I didn't think we'd get to this discussion so quickly, but now I'll have to tell you about Robert."

I said again, "You don't have to do this . . . ."

"We might as well talk about it now that you've brought those weekends up."

She went straight into it. "He was an old friend from Ohio State who I knew in the lit department. We'd dated a little around the time we were both graduating with our master's degrees. He went on to Kenyon College at Gambier to teach as an associate prof in their lit department and wanted me to go there with him. But I didn't love him enough to follow him there, and I wanted to go to Antioch, as you know."

"Kenyon is a beautiful place; did you have an offer to teach there?"

"Yes, and Dennison, and Ohio Wesleyan, and Ohio State, and even to go back to Oberlin, too."

"All really good schools, but you went to Yellow Springs to teach at Antioch. That always surprised me."

"I know. And as I told you back then, it was a mistake. Not Antioch, but moving back to my home town, Dayton. Anyway, Robert couldn't accept that I'd gone to Antioch and my living in Dayton and kept after me about it. He thought I was wasting my career."

"It was a romantic relationship then, you and Robert."

"In the beginning, yes. The first time—and I only spent a few weekends with him, mostly before I knew you well—I thought we might rekindle the old flame and I'd listen to his arguments again. There was still a little spark between us, but it seemed a lot less intense than in our OSU days. And it was clear to me after that first weekend when I went to Gambier, and the second when he came to Dayton, that it was flaming out. I couldn't put my finger on what was different until the last time I went over to Gambier. Then it hit me square in the face."

"What?"

"After a long evening with dinner at a nice restaurant, he told me he couldn't be my lover any longer. He just wanted to be friends from then on."

"Friends. How I hate that one! I heard that too many times myself. So what happened?"

"Yes, just friends. I know and I apologize for saying it to you back then. Sometimes it's the right thing for two people—but usually not—and it's depressing. Anyway, I asked him, 'Why, what's going on?' He said I wasn't sexually attractive to him anymore."

"What? Just like that?" *How the hell could that be, Dianne was one of the most sexual girls I'd ever known!*

"First I thought it was me. But then he said he had a new 'boyfriend,'" Dianne said, finger wiggling air quotes. She was silent for a short while, and then, in an emotional whisper, added, "He was throwing me over for a guy!"

"Ughhh, that had to hurt. . . ."

Bitterly, she said, "Yeah, ughhh! I was flabbergasted. I guess you always should be ready to find you've been replaced by someone prettier, sexier, richer, or whatever. But being replaced by another person of the other sex is something of a downer—not to mention shocking."

Lost for words, I stammered for a while before saying, "Well . . . yes . . . wow! That had to feel strange. But you had to understand that it wasn't anything to do with you at that point, didn't you? I mean, he was changing his sexual orientation, and you weren't the right sex. You can't take that personally; he changed and left you for a new, different lifestyle."

"Yes, wow, indeed! It jolted me and . . . and it . . . it made me feel so inadequate. And it depressed me for weeks. But then I realized that it probably wasn't suddenly a 'new and different life' at that point. It had to have been going on for quite a while because he said 'new' boyfriend," Dianne answered, using air quotes again.

"Do you think he was seeing guys when you both were still at OSU?"

"I don't really know, but it didn't seem like it. He was always hot—too hot, actually—for my tastes. He must have changed after we left OSU in the year or more that I hadn't seen him. I hope that's the case; it's too creepy to think he might have been seeing men at the same time as me."

"Maybe he was in the first phase of that change when you went over to Gambier to see him?"

"Yeah; why the hell he called me and invited me over at that point is a mystery. After it was over, thinking back about it, I hoped that was the situation. It . . . it was . . . I don't know . . . nauseating is one word for it. Like, was I interchangeable with some guy?"

"Do you think he might have been reconsidering his changing—you know—second thoughts—a last chance kind of thing?"

"Maybe. I remember hearing, when he was hanging up the phone in another room after talking to someone, him saying aloud to himself, 'This is never going to work.'"

"That was before he told you about the new boyfriend?"

"Yes, that happened later that night. We stayed up late that last night; he wanted to tell me about his new friend but I didn't want to hear about it. How could I even pretend to be interested in this new person—or about this new, fantastic thing he was experiencing? I mean I have nothing against gay men, but I have a lot against losing out to one! I tried to act interested and let him go on about it, but it was so goddamn hard trying to pretend to be happy he'd found his new future life when I was feeling like fish-wrap paper. All I could think about was getting away from him. I slept in the guest bedroom and left the next morning before he woke up. I got the hell out of that!"

"Ever see or hear from him again?"

"He called, but I hung up on him. Do you want to know something that has always bothered me about it whenever I've thought of him since then? That is, after I got over the shock of the whole thing?"

"What?"

"I've never been able to figure out which role he would have played in his new relationship."

"Strange. I'd think you would have had some clues. Don't you think he would have shown a tendency for the male or the female role that you'd have noticed?"

"Believe me, I've thought about that over and over, and have never settled on it. Actually, now I can see him in either, or both, roles."

"A switch hitter! I won't ask why, but do you really care?"

"Sometimes. Thinking back about it, I wonder about who he thought I was . . . you know? It still makes me feel very strange. Like, was he wishing I could play the man sometimes? I've never been able to shake it."

"Jesus, Dianne, no wonder you wanted to get away. I never would have guessed you were going through that. It didn't show."

"Why would I talk about that to anyone? I certainly wasn't going to tell you about it. I can put up a pretty good front."

"What about Mary? Did Mary know it?"

"Of course; we told each other everything—we were like sisters. But still, it completely threw me off balance—like I wasn't sure I could read people after that. So, that's what was happening to me when you and I first met, and then for the next couple of months. I didn't know if I could trust myself in a relationship again. If I couldn't see into people any better than I had Robert, how could I trust myself with you? I didn't need another complicated relationship at that point."

"So that was the reason you told me when we first met that you wanted to have me as a friend—and not a lover?"

"I don't think I said it that way, did I?"

"Not in so many words, but something like that. I remember you said you 'weren't putting the make on me.' I do remember those words—more than twenty years later. They've stayed with me ever since. I can still see you saying it, there in the Lamplighter."

"I just wanted someone—a good guy—to be a friend and to hang out with."

"But you wouldn't have thought I might have been . . . ?"

"You . . . gay? No, not that. It's just that I didn't have confidence in myself and felt like I needed some time to get it together. But after a while I knew who you were, and I became comfortable with you."

"Now I'm starting to wonder if that weekend we spent together was some kind of test! I mean, that last night—" I said, meaning for it to be a half-joke before she cut me off.

"Oh, come on, Tom! I think you're joking, but give me a little credit. I was already there! You came along just when I needed you."

"I'm sorry, I didn't mean to be flip about it. This has been a pretty deep conversation and I was just trying to lighten it up a little."

"I know, and I appreciate that. But, that's when I knew I wanted you coming along to California with us."

Twenty years and things were finally starting to fall into place. "Wish I'd have known all this back then."

"Would you have done anything differently, Tom? I mean, between us? Honestly?"

"I don't know. I doubt it. My reasons for staying were completely separate from all this. But who knows?"

"Exactly. You did what you had to do, and so did I. But I admit that I should have let you know that asking you to come along to California was because spending time with you is what helped me recover from that experience. I didn't know how to explain it . . . no, that's not it . . . I guess I couldn't tell anyone about how much it had hurt me. It was embarrassing and too personal. I'm sorry, I didn't deal with it like I should have."

"Neither of us did . . . ."

Not knowing what more to say, I drove on in silence, Dianne quietly staring at the conveyor belt of oncoming snowy road ahead, endlessly rolling into the Jeep's headlight pattern. The dim dashboard lighting reflected her face in my windshield, lost in thoughts and memories. I couldn't imagine the emotions running through her mind.

⁓

"So much for that question of whether you were trying—" I started to say in a pathetic attempt at a humorous way of closing that topic and trying to rekindle a new conversation.

"Yes . . . well, let's not go there! I don't want to offend your tender Ohio sensibilities with how hard I was trying out here in California." she said with a laugh.

What the hell did that mean? But I was glad she could laugh about it, and I hoped she was just putting me on a little. I changed the subject slightly. "Are you okay with how it's all turned out; I mean being single now?"

"I guess. A woman can live like I have in California and it's not a big deal. I came out here for the freedom—certainly not because I wanted to be single all my life, but for the freedom-without-questions to do that, if that's what I want to do. And for the freedoms Mary and I had. And it's not like I was 'single' either," she said with air quotes. "I don't think Mary and I ever felt like we were 'singles'. We had a strong, close relationship that kept us happy enough."

"Enough? Not completely, though?"

"Oh, Tom . . . you would ask that. Of course, not completely. Women know what women want better than men in so many ways, but there are things that can't be offered by another woman. That's the part about my 'trying' out here in California we decided to not talk about."

"Dave . . . ?"

"We'll leave it at that."

"I know. I'm sorry. Did you ever consider that your and Mary's failures with men had something to do with having each other to fall back on?"

"That probably had a lot to do with it. Keeping a close relationship going between a man and a woman can be a bitch, and maybe the easiest thing for us was just going back to each other when we hit the rough spots."

"Dianne, I think you and Mary did the right thing for yourselves. But . . . ." I stopped and wanted to pull that last word back out of the air, but it was gone.

"I already know what you're wondering. Can I have a normal relationship with a man—now . . . with you?"

I didn't say anything. After broaching the topic, I was worrying about pushing too far. I only turned to look at her with raised eyebrows: a questioning glance.

She wanted to answer the question. "The answer, Tom, is yes. With you— definitely yes. I've known it for years. I don't think I would have met you at the door if I didn't."

My heart did a double beat. "So now we're back to Mary's question again."

"You staying? Yes, and your timing is perfect, dear. I can't say that was true twenty years ago, but it's a lot better now."

Dear! How did we—I—let it get away? Dylan always had the right words: *Where you been don't bother me or bring me down in sorrow, It don't even matter to me where you're wakin' up tomorrow . . . .*

The Jeep easily finished the slow climb up snowy Rt. 50. We were a short distance from Tahoe, and then, hopefully, Whiskey Creek, the Falcons—and Suze.

Tahoe

"Harrah's marquee has a 'VACANCY' up. Let's stay there," I said as we drove along the main drag in South Tahoe.

"Good idea. They'll probably have a maître-de or bellman who know their way around Tahoe's bars and joints. Or there might be a local bar band playing who we can ask about Whiskey Creek."

"Yes, we'll probably do as well here as anywhere with our questions. It's ten o'clock and Whiskey Creek should still be open for a couple of hours. Are you up for checking it out yet tonight?"

"Are you kidding? I'm wide freaking awake," Dianne said. "And I don't want to let this drag out. I'm worried about those guys in the band, and I'm starting to worry about her aunt and uncle. Suze's comment about Mike getting a little weird bothers me. I'd like to find her and get her to a safe place tonight."

We approached the front desk. "One room or two? I'm paying for whatever you'd like," I said.

Dianne looked at me with a why-are-you-asking-me-that look. "One. Why would we get two now?"

"Okay, one bed, or two?"

"Why do I have to make these decisions?" she asked with fake sarcasm, placing an arm around my waist and hip-bumping me.

"Just being a gentleman. What's available?" I asked the desk clerk.

"We only have suites with double queens. There's a kitchenette and a sitting room that has a folding sofa-bed," was the answer.

"We like it. Here's my card."

"Yes, we've got options," Dianne said with a wink at the smiling, curious young lady.

⌐⌐→

"I want to know about a place called Whiskey Creek," I told the bellman as he waited for his tip. I gave him a twenty and told him there'd be another twenty if he came back with information on the place in fifteen minutes. He looked surprised, happily nodding his head, "Yes sir. I've heard of the place but have never been there. I'll be right back."

We unpacked our hurriedly thrown together bags and sat on the couch, waiting for our bellboy. Dianne unfastened the clip holding her pony tail and shook her head to let her hair fall around her shoulders and down her back. The stress of the recent days showed a tired face, that, even after the life events she'd described to me in the last few hours, was the face of a still remarkably lovely, mature woman.

"My God, Tom. I can't believe everything that's happened in the last several days. Are there any other surprises coming?"

"I hope only good ones. We made it across the Sierra in a snowstorm and heard from Suze and where to find her. It seems like things are going our way."

"Yes, but I don't trust fate. It's always seemed to turn out to be the fickle finger for me," she said with a pouty grimace. "I'm ready for some good news."

There was a knock on the door. The bellman arrived with the information we were hoping to hear. Whiskey Creek was several miles north and west of South Tahoe on Highway 89, at the rear of a little cluster of tourist businesses just before Emerald Bay. It was a thirty-minute drive: across town and then north on the two-lane highway, assuming the road was cleared of snow.

I gave him the twenty and we hurried to the elevator.

The Falcons

$\mathcal{W}$hiskey Creek was a long, low ranch-style building with a wood-planked porch running its full length, flanked by a hand railing on the parking lot side that reminded me of horse hitching rails. It could have been a place out of an old western movie where you expected to see men with whiskey-filled shot glasses next to their stacks of money, playing poker in a room full of round-topped tables, and saloon girls leaning against a room-length bar eying every man walking through double swinging doors. But there were no horses tied to the railing, drinking from water troughs; the parking lot was filled with pickup trucks and SUVs. Inside, instead of poker tables, there were bare wood, picnic-style dining tables to one side of the entry area and rows of bench seats arranged theater style filling the opposite end. The benches were separated from a raised stage by a small dance floor. Electronic video games, pool tables, shuffle board, and other bar-room type games filled an open area on the other side of the U-shaped bar. The players were mostly noisy young men in boots, jeans and flannel shirts. Everything inside of Whiskey Creek was made of knotty pine: the floors, the walls, the bar, the tables, the unpadded bench seats, and a stairway leading to the stage. Even the ceiling was knotty pine.

A full-house crowd of middle-aged men and women, nearly all wearing jeans and boots, filled the bench seats. On stage were The Falcons, singing the Eagles' "Already Gone" as we entered the building. The dance floor was packed with people dancing and singing: *and you can eat your lunch all by yourself,* while they shuffled, trying to keep from maiming other dancers. It was mostly dancing in place in little, hobbled country-swing and Texas Two Step dance moves.

Suze, dressed in tight jeans, spikey heels and a sparkling burgundy sequined top, stood behind the bass player on a raised platform, well off to the side of the drummer with her own microphone, joining in on vocals when the tune hit the refrain: *And me, I'm already gone, and I'm singing this song, woo hoo hoo, woo ho ho . . . .*

This was a different Suze than the girl in a pink top, long-sleeve shirt, pink tennis shoes and straw hat I'd picked up in Kansas. There was a huge smile on her face as she did a little dance number between refrains, shaking and hitting her hip with a tambourine in time to the beat. Different, but not unexpected: Suze looked like she was born to be on stage and having the time of her life. She didn't see us, as we edged along an aisle way near the wall, stopping at the rear of the bench seating area.

Dianne and I found standing room there, along the wall, behind the audience. We had to look around a group of guys drinking beers and jumping into and blocking our view every few minutes. They didn't look sober enough for a conversation about good audience manners, so we let it go and waited for the show to end at midnight. We'd arrived at 11:30 pm and wanted to wait until the show ended and then go up to the stage to signal Suze to let us meet with her.

"Is that her, Tom? Is that Suze? My Suze? Oh, my God, look at how pretty she is. Oh Tom, I want to cry . . . ." Tears were already rolling down her cheeks.

"That's her, hon. That's our daughter."

"Oh, Tom, I just want to go up on that stage and hug her."

"I know, I do too." I thought about the kiss she'd planted on my cheek the night I left her in San Diego. "But it'll only be a little while before they're done."

The lead singer, Ronnie, thanked the audience for their applause after finishing "Already Gone" and introduced the next number.

"Folks, the next tune was not an Eagles number, but you could say it almost was. It's a number originally written and sung by Roy Orbison and later made popular again by the Eagles' friend, Linda Ronstadt. Back then, she sometimes sang with the Eagles, and they sometimes sang with her as backup vocalists, or playing in her band. It's going to be sung for you tonight by a new member of the Falcons: Suze, a young lady we just met in San Diego who knocked us out last night when she showed us how to sing the high parts that, I have to admit, we weren't doing very well."

"Ladies and gentlemen, this is 'Blue Bayou,' sung by Suze Arnold!"

Suze stepped to the center microphone, showing only a little nervousness, and without hesitation hit the opening lines a cappella: *I feel so bad I've got a worried mind, I'm so lonesome all of the time, since I left my baby behind . . .* before the band came in with bass and drums, followed by the slide guitar. Her every note was perfect, right on the downbeat with precise coordination between musicians and singer. As she finished the song, Suze hit the incredible ending notes Linda made so famous with her pitch-perfect, huge vocal range. It was a show stopper, and the audience sprang to its feet in a rousing standing ovation.

"How did you like that?" I asked a speechless Dianne.

"Oh my God, Tom, where did she get that? I can't sing a note!"

"Me either. She told me she sang a little in glee club in school, and her church choir. But you don't learn to do that in glee club or church."

"I can't wait to talk to her . . . . But, I'm still afraid she isn't going to like me. Please be careful when you introduce us, so she isn't shocked."

"She's going to be shocked no matter what I say or how I say it. I'm just going to say that I have someone you're going to want to meet and get to know, and then let things take their natural course."

Dianne frowned and gulped, swallowing hard, "Shit, Tom, I don't know if I can do this. For a person who thinks she's in control most of the time, I'm panicking."

I put my arm around her waist, "You're too cool for that."

"Cool? I think I'm going to wet my pants!"

Ronnie told the audience how much the band appreciated their applause and love of Eagles music, then introduced the final number for the evening: "Hotel California." The Falcons eased into the opening twelve-string guitar lead-in and the audience went wild. They sang the song once, and for an encore, sang it again from the mid-song guitar solo. Suze sang the high parts of the refrains along with the rest of the band, shaking her tambourine and swinging her body with the rhythm. She had been born for it.

With the audience going wild, standing, whistling, and hooting for more, the Falcons took multiple bows, and as the stage darkened, they walked off toward the steps and exit door.

I pulled Dianne along by her hand as we tried navigating our way upstream through the crowd that was pushing its way back toward us, heading for the front door. By the time we got to the steps at the side of the stage, we had to look around well-wishers' heads and through the open stage door to see that the band had left the building and were moving through the parking lot to their white Suburban. We bulled our way through the door and I yelled Suze's name at the top of my voice. She looked around to see who was calling her. As I waved my hands so she could see who was calling, she recognized me and waved back. But as she started back towards us, a figure came from behind and wrapped his arms around her, pulling her backwards along with him as he backed toward a black SUV waiting with a rear passenger door open. Another figure was in the driver's seat. Terrified, Suze was shoved into the SUV's back seat. The figure, a man I then recognized as Mike Baldwin, jumped into the rear seat beside Suze, slammed the door shut, and the driver accelerated away.

"Jesus Christ, it's Mike and Julie! Now we know why they never answered their phone; they've been chasing her too."

"Where are they going with her?" Dianne screamed.

"I don't know, maybe back to San Diego. But I don't like it." I remembered what she said about Mike acting weird and that she didn't trust him.

"Yes, I was thinking the—"

"We've got to follow them. I'm going for my car."

"You'll never get it in time. Look, Tom, one of the band guys is jumping into that white Suburban." The SUV, without its trailer, which had been unhitched and left sitting next to the stage door, was starting and the headlights flashed on.

"Run, Dianne. Let's get in with him, he's probably going after them."

We flagged the Suburban down just as the driver was about to leave the parking spot. He looked like he wanted to run over us where we'd stopped in front of the vehicle.

"Get the fuck out of my way, idiots!"

"Wait, we're Suze's parents. We have to go with you!"

He looked at us like we were crazy, but then said, "Hurry the fuck up, or we'll lose them."

I jumped into the front passenger seat beside the driver, who turned out to be Jimmy, the drummer. Dianne got into a rear seat, and Ronnie, the lead singer, opened the other rear door and slid onto the back seat with her. Jimmy blasted out of the parking lot, following the black Ford Explorer that had run the red light at the parking lot driveway's intersection with Highway 89. They were heading back toward downtown Tahoe in a light but increasing snowfall.

"Who the hell are you people?" Jimmy asked.

"We're Suze's parents. We're not the people she ran away from; they are," I said, pointing at the black Ford Explorer. "It's a long story, but she's our child who we haven't seen since she was born."

"She told us she was running away from an aunt and uncle she didn't trust," Ronnie said.

"We know. She left messages on my car phone about it. She said Mike, the man who grabbed her, was getting very weird, and she had to get away."

"So you must be Mr. Patterson? Tom, the guy she came across country with?" Ronnie asked.

"Yeah, I am. Look, we're here to help her. Trust us and let's drop it for now so we don't lose them."

"Okay. There they are, running another light up there," Jimmy said.

"You're going to have to run it too," I said.

"What the fuck is a little red light," he said as he looked both ways and accelerated on through.

We followed them into South Tahoe city that way; the Explorer just making it through yellow lights, leaving us to run the red lights, or both cars running red lights, driving at fifty and sixty miles per hour in twenty-five and thirty-five miles per hour zones. It was a miracle neither car had an accident at those intersections or on the slippery, slush-covered streets. A cop in a patrol car stopping them, or both of us, would have been a good thing, but we had no such luck.

Staying behind them by several car lengths allowed us to remain in close contact, but not too close. Jimmy smartly realized they were likely to try luring us into an intentionally set up rear-end accident by suddenly braking hard when we didn't expect it and then accelerating away, leaving us with a damaged front end or engine and unable to continue the chase. With that trick failing multiple times, Julie turned the Explorer through three right turns, circling a city block, and then made a left turn back onto the highway, going back north, heading again toward Emerald Bay.

As both cars moved out of town, we encountered roadway becoming even more slippery because of deeper snow and less traffic. It looked like it hadn't been plowed for several hours. Route 89's elevation continued to rise going northbound as we approached Emerald Bay, with the snow cover becoming an even more worrisome problem. Mile by mile, it was getting worse: both cars slipping and sliding, but neither driver slowing. Julie's snow driving was poor and showed all the signs of an inexperienced bad weather driver: braking too hard and steering too sharply, then gassing the engine too much after pulling out of the last skid. Jimmy swore he wouldn't lose her because of his experience driving in Michigan snows before moving to California two years earlier. His smooth driving made me a believer.

I thought we were doing pretty well, but all we could do was follow them. How the hell we would safely overtake and stop them was the question. Either we followed them like that until someone ran out of gas, or had an accident, or something happened that would change the circumstances.

I was worried about the drop off from either side of the roadway, which ran along a high, narrow ridge separating two bodies of water. Emerald Bay, down a steep slope on my side, was visible far below in the reflection of the moon peeking through rare openings in the cloud layers. Cascade Lake was also visible below the other side of the road, down an even steeper slope—not a good place for driving mistakes. The only sound from Dianne and Ronnie in the rear seats was an occasional, frightened, "Shit, look out, Jimmy!"

It had to be worse for Suze, riding in a car driven by a poor bad-weather driver who was basically out of control. I was having visions of the black Explorer sliding off one side of the road or the other and disappearing down one of those long slopes into cold, black water.

And then that vision happened: The Ford slid to the right side of the road toward Emerald Bay. It glanced off the guardrail as Julie corrected the steering but over-corrected, and the SUV shot to the other side of the road, hit the low steel guardrail nearly head-on, and bounced completely over. The Explorer disappeared down the slope toward Cascade Lake. The last things we saw as we slid by, braking as hard as the snow-covered road allowed, were the Explorer's bouncing red taillights as it bounded over the uneven, snow-covered soil and rocks, heading down into the darkness.

"Oh fuck! Jesus Christ, Tom, they went over!" Dianne screamed.

Jimmy did a great job of slowing the car to a stop without losing control and backed up to the spot where the Ford had disappeared over the badly bent guardrail. We jumped out of the car, staring at the Explorer dozens of yards down the slope, lights on and smashed against a tree. There was no sound and no movement. We saw the final, dying exhaust fumes drifting out and up from the tail pipe. The engine had probably stalled when the tree jammed the front-end sheet metal back against the engine's accessory pumps and pulleys.

"I don't see anyone moving around in the car. Everyone must be knocked out," Ronnie said. "How the hell do we get down there? It's too steep and too slippery to try hiking down there."

I had to try something. "I'm going. I'm going to try sliding on my butt and use my feet as brakes to try to get down without sliding past the car."

"But how the hell are you going to get back up?" Jimmy asked.

"I have no idea, but I've got to try. Do you have a rope in the car?"

"Yeah! Hell yeah!" Jimmie yelled. "Ronnie, get the rope from the spare tire compartment." Looking back at me, he added, "But I don't know if it's long enough."

"Tie it to the guardrail and throw the loose end down as far as it'll reach," I told him. "And if you have any road flares or emergency lights, get them lit up!"

Cascade Lake

*S*liding down the steep slope was easier said than done. In places, the snow was too powdery to offer any braking, and in others, it was too shallow and my feet hit rocks and ruts in the soil. At one place, just after hitting thin snow that didn't give me enough footing for braking, I gained too much speed and hit ruts that stopped my feet and flipped me up and over in a full somersault. After the flip, I struggled to regain my balance and get my feet back in front of me again. Finally, regaining control, I found myself sliding on a course that would take me past the Explorer with next to no way of getting back uphill to my target. I managed to brake to a halt and crawled sideways across the slope, going slightly uphill to finish a few feet above the vehicle. I took a minute to look things over before continuing down to the car.

The Explorer had hit the tree with its center-right front end and was sitting at a forty-five-degree angle on the hillside. It didn't look like a stable situation; the back of the Explorer could slip and rotate a few degrees at any time which would probably be enough to start it sliding on down the slope to the lake. A rescue had to happen quickly.

Suze popped up in the back seat, face to the door window, mouthing something to me. She looked terrified with her situation, but thrilled to see me, her face showing fear in her eyes and yet a tight smile of hope. She was pointing at something and watching me to see if I understood what she was trying to tell me.

Thank God, she looks okay! From her motions and by reading her lips I realized she was trying to tell me the doors were locked.

Of course, Julie would have used the child power lock in the front driver-side door to lock all the doors so she couldn't escape. Suze was locked in a car that at any minute might start slipping and resume its death slide into the lake.

I needed to do something fast. In the final seconds I spent appraising the situation, I heard scuffing sounds behind me. In a flurry of snow and curse words, Jimmy slid into me, almost knocking me over and sending us both crashing into the precariously balanced Explorer.

"Fuck! I almost killed myself! Hey Tom, how are we gonna do this?" he asked, out of breath.

"She's locked in but looks okay. I don't see any sign of Mike, and Julie is slumped over the steering wheel. I can't tell if they're dead or alive. But we've got to move fast before that thing starts sliding around the tree."

"Okay. First thing we do is get to the front passenger door and see if we can open it. If it's locked too, we're gonna' have to break a window to get in and release the lock. We don't want to go around to the downhill driver's door and be beneath that thing if it starts to slide, so it's gotta' be the passenger front door."

I carefully inched my way to the front passenger door and found it was also locked. Suze was trying to reach over the front seat back to try unlocking the door but was unable to reach it.

I screamed, "Stop!" at her. "Don't shift your weight around in the car! You might make it start slipping."

With a terrified look, she nodded her head and eased backward into her seat.

"We have to carefully break the door glass, Jimmy. But I don't have a clue about how to do it. What do you have in the Suburban? Do you have a hammer?"

"Naw, man. We don't have anything but guitar and keyboard cases in there. There's a tire wrench, but it's pretty wimpy."

"How the hell are we going to break through auto glass? It's hard as steel."

"These," Jimmy said, pointing to his boots.

His boots were western style boots with glistening, pointed steel tips.

"Okay, that might work if you can swing hard enough." I said.

"Swing hell! Kick! I'm gonna use a karate kick I learned in martial arts training."

"Yes," I yelled. "Let's try it.!"

We changed positions to allow Jimmy enough room to set his body for the karate kicks. I moved to the rear door where Suze was worriedly smiling at us and gesturing toward the front seats. She was saying, "The lock is up there." I nodded and yelled at her to be cool and not move. She understood and clasped her hands in a prayer-like grip. Her muffled words were saying, "I love you, I love you . . . ."

Jimmy had moved into position facing the passenger door pillar and was practicing karate kicks by leaning as far to his left as his balance and the snowy slope would allow, propping against himself against the slope with his left arm, and then at half speed, kicking upward toward the window with his right foot, but without touching it. He was trying to get his balance and distance right before launching the real thing. After a few of the practice kicks and positioning himself slightly behind the door and two feet uphill, he paused to look over at me, saying, "Here goes!"

Before he let loose with his first kick, I said, "Jimmy, you have to use kicks that have a sharp impact but that don't let your body weight come into contact with the car. You can't add any weight to it or you might start it sliding. It's got to be a sharp, clean, but not heavy impact. Does that make sense?"

"Fuck'n A man! It's got to be all about a sharp impact and then back off, right?"

"You got it. Sounds easier than it'll be though."

"No, that's how I learned to bust store windows without getting cut back in Detroit. Street smarts, man."

Jimmy launched his first kick, but his left foot slipped and he fell on his back, missing everything. "Fuck!"

He got back up and readied himself for another kick. That one hit its mark, but didn't break the glass. It was a glancing blow without enough force to break through. With a determined look and a yell, "This one will fucking get it," he launched another kick.

The glass shattered as Jimmy's foot rebounded off the shattered door window. We both screamed "Yes!" Jimmy raised himself off the snow and picked out the rest of the glass pieces that had shattered but hadn't fallen and were still rimming the edges of the window frame. He reached through the open window and fished around, trying to find the lock in the armrest panel.

"Shit, where the hell is it?"

Suze found the ceiling lamp switch and turned it on to help Jimmy, who had his head through the door and over the passenger seat, looking frantically for the switch. As he added his body weight by laying his stomach across the window sill, the Explorer lurched a tiny amount. It was an almost invisible amount, but Suze and Jimmy felt it. The rear tires had slipped an inch or two farther downhill.

"Oh shit, it's moving!" Suze yelled.

"I know, but just a tiny amount. Stay still! Jimmy, try to find that switch and click it without moving your body, just move your arms," I said as calmly as possible, my heart trying to beat its way out of my chest.

"Okay, I think this is it." We all heard the click.

Carefully, I opened the rear door and untangled Suze's seat belt, grabbed her arms, and hurriedly pulled her through the door. I lost my footing and she came out, falling on top of me. In nearly the same instant, Jimmy had extracted himself from the window and fallen onto his back, three feet away from us. The car slipped another inch or two.

Suze lifted herself off me and rolled to my side, onto her back. "Oh God, I'm so glad to see you guys! You saved my life! I was afraid the car was going to slide down into the lake!"

"Hi honey," I said. "We have to see about Julie and Mike; let's get up."

"I don't care about them," she answered.

"I know, but we can't just leave them."

Jimmy joined the conversation, saying, "Julie looks bad. A lot of blood came out her nose and mouth and I didn't see any movement or signs of breathing. There didn't seem to be any air bubbling through the blood. I couldn't see much more because the airbag was covering everything below her shoulders."

When I had reached in for Suze, I had noticed that Mike was slumped into the bloody rear-seat's foot well, doubled up with just his behind still on the seat. Blood had run from his scalp onto everything, and he was not moving. His side window was shattered from the impact with his head. His unused seatbelt was still fully wound in its retainer.

"Okay, I don't see how to get them out any way that's safe for us if they aren't able to help us. They'll be dead weight and impossible to pull up and out of there. We shouldn't go into the car; it's still slipping and the risk of disturbing it and sending it sliding down the slope is too great. We're going to have to get professional rescuers' help for that. Let's try to get up to the car," I said.

Ronnie and Dianne had tied the long plastic rope to a guardrail post and thrown the loose end downhill toward us. It was too short by roughly twenty feet, but Ronnie had a plan. He'd already slid and stumbled, holding onto the rope, down the hillside to a tree where the rope ended.

"I'm down as far as I can go," he yelled. "I'll wait here and you two try to get Suze up here where I can grab her hands. If you can do that, I'll tie the rope around her waist and maybe with me behind her and Dianne pulling from the top, we can get her back up to the road."

We inched our way up toward Ronnie, sliding back one foot for every two feet we'd gain. Suze had ditched her high heels and was making the climb in bare feet and her sleeveless, sequined top, suffering badly from the freezing snow. If we didn't get her up to the roadway soon, frostbite would be a possibility. Gradually we came up to where Ronnie grabbed Suze's hands and pulled her up to the tree with him.

"I don't see how you're going to be able to keep your footing and push her up that last steep part, Ronnie," I said. "And I don't think Dianne will be strong enough to take much weight off for you."

"I know; that's what I'm worried about. All I can do is try, man. Here goes!"

It didn't go well. Suze's bare feet had almost no traction, slipping continually and getting painful scrapes and bruises from the rough terrain when they pushed through in places where the snow cover was thin. After fifteen minutes, it was clear the plan would fail.

"Keep trying, guys," Dianne yelled from the road. "You're halfway up!"

"I'm exhausted; let me breathe a minute," Ronnie answered.

Terrified of losing her daughter before she had a chance to even meet and touch her, Dianne yelled, "Suze, you've got to make it! I'm Dianne, your real mother, baby! Come on, keep trying. Please!"

"What are you talking about? How can that be?" an astonished Suze yelled back.

"I gave birth to you in Salina, Kansas in 1968! I gave you up for adoption but made the family promise to name you Suze. That's why you have your name!"

"Mom! You're my real mom? How did you get here?"

"Tom was bringing me to meet you. He's your real dad!"

"You're not kidding me are you? This is crazy! You've got to be kidding!"

"Ask Tom, honey!"

As she turned to look back down the hill to where Jimmy and I were standing, I yelled, "It's true! My Dianne is your mom. We'll explain it when we're back up to the car."

Stunned, but energized by what she'd just heard, and without another word, Suze frantically began pulling herself uphill, hand over hand on the rope, feet slipping, and at times falling face down in the snow. Ronnie scrambled uphill, reaching her just as they arrived at the steepest part, thirty feet below the guardrail. There they stopped making progress. The slope was too steep and Dianne's strength wasn't enough to help them.

"Oh shit! Come on, don't stop now," Dianne yelled at them. "You can make it!"

"We can't," Ronnie yelled back.

"Don't let go. You can't drop back now. Hang on!" Dianne yelled, encouraging them to keep trying.

"I don't think I can do this," Suze yelled back. "My feet are freezing and I can't feel anything with them. I don't even know when they're in the snow or out of it," she answered with anguish in her voice.

"Baby, please keep trying!"

"I am . . . Mom . . . !"

The first passing car that had finally seen the emergency flares came onto the scene just then and stopped behind the Suburban. Two men jumped out and asked if they could help.

"Oh Jesus, yes; we could use some help! A car went over the guardrail with three people in it," Dianne said, pointing down at us, "We're trying to get this girl up here to safety. She may be the only one who survived. Can you help me pull her up here?"

"Yes mam!"

They pulled—dragged—Suze up to the guardrail where Dianne grabbed her and wrapped her in a tight embrace and burst into tears, "Oh Suze, honey! I've found you. I've found you after all these years."

"Thank you, thank you all! Are you really my mother? How can this be happening?"

"Come over to the car so we can get something on your feet. We can talk in there. Boys, please help get the others up, will you?"

"Yes mam. We can do it!"

One of the men went to their Jeep Wrangler, which was fitted out with spotlights, a winch on the front bumper, huge wheels and tires, and extra gas cans. He turned the spotlights on us and came running back with a very long, thick rope. They tied one end around the stoutest man's waist and tossed the other end down to the three of us. The man with the rope around his waist braced himself against the guardrail, and with their combined strength, they pulled us, one at a time, slipping and sliding, up to the guardrail. We were all back up to the road in twenty minutes. One of our rescuers dashed back to the Jeep, where they had a Citizen's Band radio he used to call for emergency help.

Dianne had helped Suze into the rear seat of the Falcon's Suburban, where she'd cleaned the blood from her feet and wrapped them in towels for warmth. When I arrived, her wrapped feet were in Dianne's lap, with Suze stretched across the seat, covered with a blanket and leaning back against the opposite door. They were both crying and trying to talk through tears.

"It's true, honey. If you were born on April sixteenth, 1968 in Salina, Kansas, and then adopted, you've got to be my daughter, Suze. And Tom is your father."

"Is it true? I can't believe this."

"Believe it, sweetie," I said.

"How did you find this all out?" Suze asked.

"I located Dianne up north of Monterey a few days ago. When we were talking about you—before we knew who you are—Dianne told me the real reason she'd interrupted her move to California was that she found out she was pregnant when she and her friends were going through Kansas. She stayed there with an aunt and uncle until the baby—you—were born. When she told me that she'd pleaded in the adoption agreement that your new parents use the name Suze, I realized that the girl I had just driven across the country had to be her daughter. But I didn't know that you'd also be my daughter until Dianne told me I was the father of that baby she left in Kansas. That's how we realized you are *our* Suze.

"This is like a movie, or a fairy tale! Dianne . . . Mom . . . sorry, I'm confused. You said you'd 'finally' found me. What did that mean? Have you been looking for me?"

"Not in a literal sense, honey. But every single day, I've wondered how you are, who you've turned out to be, and what your life has been like. And are you married, do you have a career . . . ? I cried inside every time I thought about you. But I wasn't supposed to try to find you. It was discouraged because the adoption people don't want to put the child through the torture of trying to decide . . . you know, what if . . . ?"

"But why weren't you two together in Kansas?"

Neither of us had an immediate answer, and we left the question hanging there. Sirens had been sounding in the distance for the past several seconds, growing louder and closer. While we stumbled for an answer to Suze's question, one waiting for the other to try explaining it, police, fire trucks, and a team of paramedics pulled up.

"That's a long difficult story, honey. We'll talk about that after we're done with the police and can relax and take our time with it," Dianne said.

The men had pointed the Wrangler's spotlights far downhill to light up the Explorer. One of the firemen, seeing it with its lights still on, a hundred and fifty feet downhill, asked if there were still people in it.

"Yes, a woman in the driver's seat and a man in the rear seat. They're both unconscious and look badly injured. We don't know if they're alive," I answered.

Two firemen, a paramedic, and a policeman all jumped into action, sliding downhill one after the other on the two ropes. As the first fireman approached the Explorer, the rear end again slid a small amount downhill, pivoting the car farther around the tree. The slight amount of movement started the disconnection. When the car had lurched that small amount and then stopped, the rear passenger door I'd left wide open slammed shut, hitting the door frame with a hard thud. The impact was enough to start the SUV's back end sliding more, increasing the downhill rotation. This time it didn't stop. The entire car pulled away from the tree and started backing down the slope. It hit ruts or large rocks under the snow that started it into a series of sideways rollovers that didn't stop until the vehicle went into the lake, upside down, partly submerged, with its spinning wheels above the shallow water. Lights still on, bubbles coming from the broken front window as the water poured in, the Explorer became a ghastly tomb for Julie and Mike.

With no possible way of getting themselves and any rescue equipment down to the lake shore fast enough, the emergency team realized they were no longer looking at a rescue, but a recovery effort.

Promise

*I*t was after seven am the next morning before we returned to the hotel. We'd spent several hours with the police going over Suze's story and the accident. They were skeptical until we told them to call the San Diego police to check on my reports of a missing girl and the Denny's restaurant scene. The stories were verified by the SDPD and the Denny's night manager, who had still been on his shift. But they were most interested in what was happening between Suze, Julie, and Mike, "Tell us about what was going on when he grabbed you at Whiskey Creek and dragged you into the Ford. What was that all about?"

We all listened as Suze told her story.

"I ran away because I realized that if I stayed any longer something bad would happen. The first or second day I was with them, I noticed Mike always watching me from a chair in the family room that let him look into my bedroom if I left the door open. After seeing him doing that a few times, I started keeping the door closed. But whenever I went out to cross the hallway to use the bathroom, or go into the kitchen, he'd still be there, watching. It felt creepy, but I tried to not let it bother me. Then, in another day or two, a few times when I went into the hallway, he'd get up from that chair and come into the hallway and brush up against me as he walked past. There was enough room for both of us to get through, so he didn't need to do that. It was intentional. I didn't know what to do about it, and I didn't want to mention it to Julie and start a hassle between the three of us. I was starting to realize I'd have to leave as soon as I found a job and a place to live."

Suze paused for a deep breath, wiped a tear from her eye and continued. "The day I left—the day before yesterday—I had been out at the pool doing a little sun-tanning, lying on the far side of the pool by the wall. I was on my stomach, face-down. Suddenly I felt a hand on my back and heard Mike saying, 'You need to be careful you don't get a burn on that pale Kansas skin of yours. I'll put a little lotion on it for you.' Suddenly I felt him unsnap my top, and his hand pushed me down while his other hand reached into my bottom."

Suze began to cry, but after a minute, continued, "I screamed at him and rolled off the other side of the lounge and ran into the house with my top off and my bottom hanging down around my legs. I locked myself in my bedroom and got dressed as fast as I could. I didn't know what to do, but I didn't want to stay there and have him break into my room and rape me or something. So, I opened my window and crawled out into the side yard and ran across the street, where there was a little park-like area with benches and playground stuff. I hid in a clump of bushes there for the rest of the afternoon, expecting to see Mike come looking for me. But he didn't come out to the front side of the house, so I stayed there until I saw Julie come home. There were loud voices in the house for a while, but I couldn't understand what they were yelling at each other about. Then they came out together and looked around, up and down the street. I managed to stay out of their sight until they went back into the house. There was a lot more yelling, and then around ten minutes later they backed out of the garage in the Explorer and drove up the street, going slowly, looking for me."

Suze took a few seconds to breathe and organize her thoughts, then finished the story, "I realized I might have time to get back in the house using the bedroom window. I figured I could throw my things in my suitcase and get out before they came back. That was around seven pm. I knew how to get down to the hotel and restaurant area from the house, and I took a roundabout way and hid behind bushes and parked cars whenever I saw any cars driving on the streets. I went to the hotel's coffee shop, in the back part on the main floor. It's out of sight from the street and parking lot, where I had privacy and time to try to figure out what to do. I figured a girl pulling a suitcase wouldn't look out of place doing that in the hotel. I stayed in there, drinking

Cokes until I decided to try calling Mr. Patterson. I think you know the rest of the story from there."

"You must have been terrified, honey," Dianne said, tears in her eyes, too. "Did you call your family in Kansas?"

"No, there wasn't anything they could do for me. And I wasn't going to do that; I didn't want them telling me how I'd screwed up and I didn't know what I was doing. Even if it was true, I didn't need to go through that."

Another member of the Tahoe police force walked into the room, motioned the detective to the side, and had a short conversation with him before leaving.

"Suze, we've cross checked the restaurant story with the band members and are satisfied with your explanation. The recovery team called in from the lake and confirmed Julie and Mike are dead. This story ends here with this being reported as a highway accident and nothing more if you want. There's no way, or reason, to press charges against dead people. We do have to include what you've told us in the accident report, but that's as far as it needs to go."

Suze nodded her head, saying, "It's okay with me."

The detective asked how to notify next of kin.

"I can't give you any information about Mike's family, and Aunt Julie's mom and dad—my adopted grandfather and grandmother—have both been dead for a couple of years. The only person I can help you with is my adoption mom, Julie's sister, in Kansas, Jean Arnold."

She gave the Tahoe police the phone number in Salina and we all waited while the detective made the call. Suze asked to be allowed to talk to her mom after the detective finished telling her about her sister's and brother-in-law's deaths. The detective agreed, and after giving Jean the bad news and asking for verification that she had a daughter named Suze Arnold, told her she was with him and wanted to talk to her.

"Hi mom, it's me. I'm so sorry I have to talk to you like this after leaving home, and now with Julie and Mike both dead. I was hoping things were going to be okay after we talked the other day. I want to tell you what happened."

We all heard the sobbing, loud voice, nearly screaming. Suze tried her best to calm her down and explain why she'd left Julie's house and about the accident, but she couldn't finish a sentence before there was more yelling and crying. Jean was talking so loud Suze had to hold the receiver away from her ear. We could all hear both sides of the conversation: "No, I don't want to talk to Dad. It'll just be worse. Look, I'm twenty-two and it was time for me to move away from home and Salina—and Danny . . . ."

Danny . . .? What about Danny? I wondered.

The loud voice on the other end of the call softened, but we still heard the crying.

In an emotional burst, Suze said, "I had to leave Julie and Mike's house, Mom! Mike was getting too weird with me when Julie wasn't around. I didn't trust him anymore; I think he's some kind of pervert. I don't know how Julie could stand him. He may have been trying to rape me the other day, so I ran away to try to figure out what to do. I was lucky and met a band coming up here to Tahoe who gave me a ride. I figured I could get a job up here as just as easily as in San Diego. But Mike and Julie found out where I went somehow and followed us, and then tried to kidnap me. Julie was driving when they were trying to escape with me and lost control on a snowy road."

By the end of the story, Suze was crying and hunched over in her chair, hair falling over her face and shoulders, completely miserable.

"Why, what were they going to do with you?" Jean demanded.

Through her tears, she replied, "I don't know, Mom. They were arguing about it. Julie kept saying she wasn't going to lose me on her watch. She asked me why I'd run off, and I said, 'Ask Mike.'"

"So, she turned around to look into the back seat and asked Mike what that meant. 'You're not doing that again, are you?' He said, 'Don't listen to her, she's making shit up.' And then he said, 'I want her away from us. Keep driving out 89 toward the north shore.' Julie asked, 'Why do you want to go way up there; that's not the way to San Diego.' Mike told her to 'shut up and drive faster and fucking concentrate on getting away from the car that's chasing us.' They started arguing, and that's when Julie lost control of the car and hit the guardrail."

We heard Jean loudly say, "I never liked that man in the first place. And I didn't want my sister marrying him. I would have warned you if you'd just—"

"Mom, don't. It doesn't help now. Look, I'm with really nice people; they're the ones who saved me after the accident."

"I don't care who they are," came the bawling, loud reply. "I want you back here, and now!"

"You can't make me do that. I'm going to start my own life out here."

"How?"

"I'll figure it out myself. I'm going to sing—"

"You'll end up a tramp!"

Dianne said quietly to Suze, "Let me have the phone, please."

With a questioning look that faded into a look of appreciation, she handed the phone to Dianne.

Dianne pushed the speakerphone button and placed the receiver back in its cradle.

"Hello Mrs. Arnold. This is Dianne Wolfe."

There was a long silence, then, "Dianne Wolfe?" Jean blustered, still loud and angry, "That sounds familiar. Why should I know that name?"

"You might; I'm Suze's birth mother. I'm the one who gave her the name Suze. You may not fully recognize my name since you were never supposed to know it, but it may be that somehow you heard it. I think you knew about my hopes you'd keep the name I wanted for her?"

Jean's sobbing giving way to angry, suspicious accusations. "What is this? Are you making this up? Are you trying to steal my daughter? You are, aren't you? You and Suze are making this up!"

"Mrs. Arnold, I put you on the speakerphone so Suze and another important person can hear us. I hope that's okay with you. No, I'm not making this up. It's true. Don't worry; she's going to be fine."

"Why should I believe you? Why should I believe anything you say? I don't know you; I can't even see you. Do you expect me to just take a stranger's word for it over the telephone? And who all is listening to this conversation?"

"The detective, Suze, and a man you don't know whose name is Tom Patterson. He's a close friend of mine and is the man who drove your daughter out here. In answer to your question, the detective has seen my identification and can vouch for me being who I'm saying I am."

"But he can't vouch for you being Suze's birth mother. How would he know anything about that?"

"Mrs. Arnold, I gave birth to Suze on Sunday, April sixteenth, 1968, at three-thirty in the morning at Salina Regional Health Center hospital. Nobody except you and just a few people there in Salina would know that."

"Well . . . ."

"Do you know a Harold and Marsha Wolfe in Salina? They are—if they're still alive—my aunt and uncle. But they'd be in their seventies now and I haven't heard anything about them for years. I stayed with them while I was pregnant. If you can find one or both, they would tell you about me living with them until I had my baby and gave her up for adoption. And they'd be able to tell you her birth date and which hospital she was born in if you want to verify this."

There was complete silence on the phone for a long time. Then, in a brittle, still-loud voice, she responded, "I don't know them, but if either is still alive, you can bet I'll find them and ask. And yes, just a few people in the world would know that. But you'd better not be putting me on. I don't want my little girl with strangers." Jean's crying grew louder again.

"That's not going to happen. She's going to be fine. I promise."

"If you really are her original mother, who is her father?"

"I think you know the birth records said, 'father unknown,' didn't they?"

Jean, weakening, admitted, "Yes, they did. But that doesn't prove anything. Many adoption babies have unknown for the father's name. You could just be making that up, too."

"Well, Mrs. Arnold, I'd like you to know that Suze's father is here with us, now. He is Tom Patterson, the man I just mentioned a minute ago. He's from Dayton, Ohio too, just like I am."

"Jesus Lord, lady. Either you've put the best lie in history together, or you're tellin' an incredible truth."

Suze's sad, teary face turned to one of hope; she leaned toward the telephone, saying, "Mom—Jean—I don't understand how this all happened, but it's got to be the truth. There are too many things that fit together for it not to be true. I can barely understand how this happened myself, but it did. We're not making this up. It's all . . . it's just . . . a twist of fate . . . ."

"Honey, baby, I want to believe you, because you've always been honest with me—but at the same time—I don't want to believe you because I'm afraid of losing you. I want the best for you, and I realize it's probably time for you to find your own life. I don't want to lose you . . . honey," Jean stuttered through more choking tears.

"You're not losing me, Mom."

Jean's crying became uncontrollable, "Oh . . . promise . . . promise me you'll take good care of yourself and try to be a good person. I . . . I can't talk, honey . . . and promise me you'll stay in touch with dad and me. I still want to be your mom . . . not Jean."

"I promise Mom, I promise. You'll always be my mom."

Dianne motioned to Suze to let her say something, "Mrs. Arnold. She's going to be a wonderful woman who'll make you proud. And please understand, we're not stealing her from you. No one is stealing anyone from anyone else. We just found each other and haven't talked at all about where she's going to live."

There was another long silence with intermittent sobbing, "She's a good girl. I'm going to hold you responsible. You better take good care of her and make sure she has a good home . . . please." Then louder, "Please!"

"Mrs. Arnold, if she wants to live with me, that's her decision. If she does, she'll have a good home and everything I can give her. But I don't know what she wants to do. Believe me; we haven't talked about it yet. We've done little more than introduce ourselves to each other after getting her out of that wreck."

"I'm glad to hear you say that, but I still feel like you're stealing my daughter."

"I understand how you feel, but look Mrs. Arn . . . Jean, I didn't drive out to Kansas and trap your daughter. She came out here on her own. The truth is, you'd already lost her the day she packed her suitcase. Or even sooner . . . . I'm sorry, I don't mean lost her; what I mean is . . . that it . . . that it's just that time in her life. Suze's going to be her own woman. And I know she'll stay in touch with you."

There was more silence on the phone line until Jean responded, "I . . . I . . . I don't have anything more to say . . . ." In a choking, unsteady voice, she added, "I'm going to go now. Suze, please stay in touch with me?"

Suze leaned close to the phone again and softly said, "Goodbye Mom. I'll call you soon, I promise. Love you." She pressed the speakerphone button, ending the call.

Looking at Dianne and me, she whispered, "That was hard. I hurt her more than I thought."

"You did very well, dear," Dianne said, giving her a kiss on the forehead.

"I guess it was a good thing I didn't get to tell her that I'm singing in a rock band."

"Yeah, that wouldn't have helped," I said. "And, Danny . . . ?"

"We need to talk about him later," she said, looking more at Dianne than me.

Explanation

Room service left the room at eight-thirty that morning, leaving tea and coffee, juices, eggs, pastries, waffles, fruits—everything anyone might want, that I'd ordered. The three of us were going to spend whatever amount of time needed, together in the suite, getting to know each other and going over years of lost ground. Suze had showered and walked barefooted into the sitting area of the suite, wearing the same clothes she'd been in at Whiskey Creek. The members of the Falcons had been released while we were still on the phone with Suze's mom, and she'd only managed to wave and mouth a "see you tomorrow" at them as they filed past our interview room. She hadn't yet had a chance to connect with them and her suitcase. Dianne was still in the jeans and long-sleeve tee shirt she'd been wearing since our drive from Sea Grass Estates.

"Hi, honey," Dianne said. "Have something from the table and we'll sit over there with Tom by the coffee table."

I was amazed at how much they looked alike: the same height, the same figures, and within a few pounds of each other. They even had nearly the same hair length. The only differences were from aging: the extra lines and crow's feet in Dianne's face and her greying hair. I realized why Suze had seemed so familiar to me back there in Kansas and on the rest of the drive: a thousand miles and several days—or was it twenty-two years?

I loved them both.

Suze filled a plate with fruit and muffins, poured a cup of coffee and they both came over to sit with me. "Are you really my mother and father? This is just too unbelievable."

"Yes, we must be. There can't be any other way of explaining this," Dianne said.

"How is it that I just happened to run into Tom on the highway in the middle of the country? It all seems like too much coincidence. Forgive me, but it seems like I have a right to be skeptical. I want to believe this, but it feels like it had to be planned in some crazy way."

"I don't blame you," I said. "Let's take it from the beginning, back to 1966 and Dayton, Ohio."

Between Dianne and I, we went through the entire story: how we met, the things we did together for a year, the decisions involved in Dianne's California trip, and my reasons for staying in Dayton. Amazingly, we both remembered it the same way and were able to fill in where the other's memory was vague. We spent hours in the room, snacking and drinking tea and coffee, reliving those years. Suze already knew most of my story, but needed to hear Dianne's. Dianne went through her California story that she'd already told me, but skipped the Jim Carver and Dave-the-musician parts, and details of her relationship with Mary. Both of us had skipped the part about the weekend trip to Indiana and the last night together at my Dayton apartment.

"So, how did I happen?" Suze asked at the point where Dianne had stopped her story.

I was searching for words—no, not words—an acceptable way of explaining that it *just happened*—one of those things . . . . I was fumbling for the right thing to say, when Dianne said, "I stayed with Tom in his apartment one weekend after we'd made a little trip to Indiana. We hadn't really been intimate before that, but surely, we were falling in love. I wanted Tom to come to California with me, and I wanted him to understand that I'd give myself completely to him. I don't know how to say it . . . I just wanted him with me. And you were born nine months later, in Kansas."

I was amazed at how Dianne could just say it like that to a person she hardly knew: no blushing, no hesitating, just the truth with no equivocating. I couldn't have said something like that to any of my children, even now. And Suze didn't seem embarrassed hearing it, either. There seemed to be a direct connection between them; they were in tune, and on the same wavelength.

"But why didn't you call Dad—Tom—and tell him about it when you stopped in Kansas? Why not get married, or just live together?"

"This is the hard part, honey. And it's going to sound stupid to you—and Tom as well. I was offended that after trying my best to interest Tom in going with me, he chose to stay in Dayton for his precious job. My pride was hurt and I wouldn't call him to ask for help. I'd decided on my course and wasn't about to back off or change it for anything."

"Even me?" Suze asked in disappointment.

"Yes, I guess that's the sad truth. I let my ego get in my way. I believed I was a modern girl and could handle anything my way and make it work."

"Look, Mom—Dianne—I had a pretty good life. Jean has been a good mom, and Steve wasn't so bad. So it turned out okay. But, Kansas? I didn't get to have a say in the matter naturally, but I sure would have rather been out here with you."

"You can't know that, honey. I might not have had the good job I had at the *Times*, and I probably wouldn't have been able to spend enough time with you. I don't know how I would have raised you in that situation."

"I bet that between you and Mary and Pete—you would have given me a good life."

"Are you mad at me, Suze? Are you bitter?"

After a long silence, she said, "No, not mad or bitter. Probably disappointed now that I know the whole story, I guess. I just wonder what it would have been like if you, both of you really, had made those decisions differently. I guess I can dream about it. It feels like a missed life."

"You don't have to dream about it. You can still have it," I said.

"What do you mean?" Suze asked.

"Yes, what do you mean?" Dianne added, looking at me.

I looked directly at Dianne and said, "We could live together as a family, if you agree. We could live in your beautiful place. Or, if you don't want to live there any longer, I can sell my house back in Dayton to help buy a different one out here."

"Is this a proposal?" Dianne asked with a prim little smile.

"It could be, but it doesn't have to be a marriage proposal. You can call it a 'domestic arrangement' if you prefer. This *is* 1990 and we're in California, right?"

"These things are usually discussed in private, Thomas. Not in front of one's daughter!"

"I'll leave the room if you want," Suze said. "That's a hard thing to talk about and decide in front of someone, especially someone you don't really know. I'll go to the other room and you can call me back in when you're ready."

"No, this time you do get to have a say in it. Will you stay with us, married or not married?" Dianne said.

"Mom . . . Dianne; I'm sorry, I don't know who to call you yet. It sounds wonderful. I don't have a place to stay now and I know I'd spend my two thousand dollars in a few weeks on a room and food. But are you sure you want me? We don't know if we'll get along. What about doing it on a trial basis—a few weeks to see how it's working out? If it doesn't work, we'll just shake hands and wish each other the best."

"I owe you so much I can't even begin to tell you how I want to make it up to you. I'm not worried about us getting along; I know enough from the last ten hours to know I want you with me. Please say you will."

Suze glanced at me with an uncertain look. "Yes, I think you should accept, Suze," I said.

"Well . . . yes then! But I do think we should look at it as a trial period. And we'll have to talk about what I can do."

"Like what?" I asked.

"School. I need to find a way to go to school. I don't want to flip burgers or have to look for a guy to marry for a career as a housewife. Is there a school nearby I can go to? Can I continue singing with the band when they get more gigs? Or another band that's based around here, maybe?"

"The answer is, yes; yes, to the school idea. There are plenty of good schools in the area; UC Santa Cruz, San Jose State, even Stanford and Berkley if you can get accepted. But none of them is in easy commuting distance from

Sea Grass Estates. We'll have to see what we can do, where you can get accepted, finances, and the other things. Singing in a band is something we'll have to discuss. I know you could do it, but is that the best thing to do with your talent?" Dianne asked.

"Okay, I'm in. But there's something else we need to talk about . . . ."

"What's that, honey?" Dianne asked.

"What does 'a whiter shade of pale' mean? Tom said you can explain it," she said with an angelic, innocent look.

"What?" Dianne looked at me. "What have you been telling this girl, Tom?"

Before I could answer, Suze said, "I'm sorry, Dianne . . . I am going to call you Dianne if you don't mind. It's an inside joke we made up. Tom said you'd probably be able to explain it to me. He said you could explain all of Dylan's and other old songs that are kinda' mysterious. So I told him that should be his opening line when he finally did find you. I'm guessing he really didn't do it, so thought I'd do it for him—just to lighten things up a little. Can you dig it?"

Dianne, frowning, looked back at me, "Can I dig it? It's a good thing you didn't!"

"I guess so! But why?"

"Let's just say that it cuts too close to the bone. That song has haunted me for the last twenty-two years."

"Haunted you . . . why? It's such a famous song; everyone loves it. It's a rock legend."

"Because it's about a girl leaving a boy behind after making love. I loved the song too, until I left you in Ohio, but then I've hated it ever since. Most people think it's about some kind of heavy drug scene with mystical meanings. But it's pretty simple; you can read the lyricist, Keith Reid's, remarks about it. He said he was just writing a song about a girl leaving a boy around the line, 'whiter shade of pale' that he'd been carrying around in his head for a while after hearing it in a different context at a party. He said he was highly influenced by Dylan's imagery and nuance and wanted to do something in the same vein."

"Yes, Dylan's songs and word use . . . . I do have a few questions I've been saving up for just you."

"We have plenty of time for that later." Dianne looked back at Suze, "Yes, please call me Dianne. So, Suze, we have an agreement; you'll be staying with us?"

"Yes. But there is one other thing we need to talk over."

"Now what, honey?"

"My baby. I'm pregnant." She turned to me. "Danny."

Proposal

"*I* just gave in."

"I guess you did, or it would have been rape. It wasn't rape was it, Suze?"

"No. But he was pushing pretty hard for it. He had been for months, but I always refused him, just because I didn't want to end up like this. I thought it would be safe though. It was just one time; can you believe it?" she said sadly. "Do you think there is such a thing as 'soft' date rape?"

Looking first at me, Dianne said, "Maybe. But it sounds like you were acquiescing. But what's the difference at this point? You don't want to go there anyway; I've seen too many court cases where it all becomes mush and ends up with no conclusion and everyone is embarrassed, and hating everyone else. But . . . once *is* enough, dear. How long?"

"A few weeks before I left home and came out here. So I'm around six or seven weeks now. I had a pretty good warning of it when I was riding out here with Tom. A test kit from the drugstore down the street from Julie's house confirmed it."

"Six weeks, so it happened in what, August?"

"Yes, the middle of August." Then she added, in a whisper, "In that damn truck," looking at her bare feet.

"The baby is due in April, then?"

"Yes, April. My own birthday month."

"I know; I already made that connection. Funny how you and I both discovered ourselves being pregnant on our way to California. Another strange twist of fate . . . . But, in his truck?"

"Yes, it was what he wanted. He didn't want to spend money on a motel not knowing if I'd go through with it. He's pretty thrifty, I guess."

"Thrifty! I'd call it cheap! It's a good thing you got away from someone like that. He didn't trust you and wouldn't even go first class! You deserved a hell of a lot better than that, my dear."

"It was awful, Mom. I was so confused; I was scared and excited at the same time. I had fear of what could happen in the back of my mind, but I'm twenty-two and had never had sex before. But it wasn't the kind of experience I always heard it would be from my friends. There was no magic carpet ride, or out-of-this-world feeling about it. My head was jammed up against the armrest and I was sliding off the vinyl seat . . . . Jesus, I can't believe I'm telling you this! I wouldn't ever have told Jean about it."

"Suze, honey, that's good. We can have a different relationship; I'm not going to be viewing you as a child. I don't have all the emotional baggage and hang-ups a mother in Kansas might have. We can talk to each other as adults. Think of me as a best friend, or a counselor, or soul mate. You don't have to feel there's an, 'I can't tell my mom about this,' thing between us. I want you to tell me everything and not worry about how I'll react. That gets in the way!"

"I'd love that. Are you sure you can treat me like that?"

"Suze, dear, look at me. I've been pregnant and unmarried, and through what you're going through, too. And I've lived out here in California for twenty-two years. I've had some affairs of my own I'm not so proud of, and have been a newspaper reporter at the *LA Times;* believe me, I've seen it all. I don't want anything other than the best for you now. And I'm not going to be holding you to any Midwestern or religious social standards."

"It sounds good, but can we really do that?"

"Let's start by talking about the baby."

"Do you want me to be here?" I asked, feeling irrelevant.

"You have to be here, Tom."

I went back to watching and listening to them, not knowing if, or how, I'd be able to contribute.

"Suze, do you want to have the baby?"

"I'm not sure; I'm all mixed up about it. It's all still so new to me that I haven't had a chance to talk to anyone. I thought about adoption, but having been through that myself, I don't know if that's what I'd do."

"Have you thought about an abortion? Understand that I'm not for or against it. I just want to know how you feel about it."

"I don't think I'd choose it, but that's really difficult. If I could pick someone to be my baby's father, it wouldn't have been Danny. I'm a little worried about that. It's not that he's a bad person, but it's more that he's not ambitious enough. He doesn't want to try breaking out of his situation for a better one. Whatever happens is okay with him, you know? He doesn't see any need to leave Salina, ever." Then she added, "I should have been more careful; I understand that. I don't want a child that turns out like Danny."

"Don't be too hard on yourself, sweetie. You were trying to use your best judgment. And you are twenty-two; most young people can't hold off that long. But is Danny intelligent? Does he have good values? Is he willing to work hard?"

"Yes, other than his lack of ambition, he's a pretty good guy."

"That can be strongly influenced by the environment a person grows up in. What are his parents like?"

"They're not like that. His dad owns a big farm equipment business and his wife teaches high school. Danny worked for his dad when he was in high school, but they couldn't get along, so he went into construction, and works on and off when things get busy in good weather."

"Then don't hold Danny's lack of ambition as something that's in the family DNA, or that will be in your baby's DNA. You hold the key to the baby's future."

"I hope you're right. I'm just lost; I don't know what I want to do."

"Suze, if you think you will want to have an abortion, do it now. Every week that goes by, it will be harder."

"I can't make that decision now. I don't know when I'll be able to think clearly enough to make a cold decision like that, if ever."

"Do you want Danny involved in this? Do you want him to have a say?"

"No. That would complicate everything too much. He's not mature enough to help with a decision like this. His ego and 'manhood' will get all wound around the axle and we won't be able to have a rational discussion about it. He'll want to get married and drag me back to Kansas and a double wide in a mobile home park. You know: it's his 'manly responsibility' . . . even though he wouldn't have a clue about how to take care of a family. I need to do this myself."

"Okay, if you decide you want to do an adoption, you have more time. But you can't let that go forever, either. There's a lot to be worked out in those arrangements."

"I know, I'd probably rather do that, if only . . . ."

"If only what, dear?"

"If only I could get to know and decide who'd be adopting the baby."

Dianne let the words hang there, silently thinking before saying, "You can make that happen." Then, looking at me, she added, "Tom, let's talk in the other room. Have some more food Suze; we might be out for a while."

Dianne and I walked into the suite's bedroom and closed the door. It didn't take long.

"I want the baby, Tom," she said.

"Yes, I could see where the conversation was going and how you're thinking."

"Are you with me?"

"How do you want to do this? As a formal adoption, or as foster parents . . . as married parents or an informal family?"

"Does it make any difference, right now—Mr. Engineer?"

"Well, it could get complicated."

"You're talking to me about complicated relationships . . . ? I think we can handle it. And haven't we both been dropping hints at each other for days now? Well?"

I hugged her and kissed her on her forehead, "Yes. Yes, I'm in. Any way you want to do it."

She placed one hand against my shoulder and gave me a long, intense kiss that told me she was sealing the agreement—and our relationship—bonding our lives.

"By the way, you can make that call now."

I knew what call she was talking about: that call to my daughter, Susan, I hadn't yet made.

"Right. But you're going to be on the call with me. I want to introduce you to my—our—daughter."

"Seems like we just did that. But, we'll do it again," she said with a smile and wink.

"I know. Like I said, it's going to get complicated."

"Piece of cake." She gave me another kiss.

"And this will be for Mary, too," I said.

"Yes, for dear Mary."

We walked back to the room, where Suze was sitting with her eyes half closed and a dazed look. "Tom and I have a proposal for you, Suze . . . ."

Sea Grass Estates - 1992

It was getting late and the surf had quieted to gentle lapping on the beach in Sea Grass Estates. Dianne was still up in San Francisco doing interviews for her newest book, *Music from Golden Gate*, about the great bands and free concerts in the park in the '60s. Suze was at UC Santa Cruz completing her freshman year in the spring of 1992, building up her academic chops before launching into a hoped-for major in literature and a minor in music—or maybe the other way around . . . . She had my entire collection of '60s and '70s vinyl albums with her.

One-year-old Joanie (Arnold-Wolfe-Patterson), sat on my lap, trying to touch Billy Blaze as I moved him around on the screen, dodging the Vorticons. It was close to her bedtime but I needed to listen to one last old song coming up next on the CD player before taking her to bed:

May you build a ladder to the stars, and climb on every rung, may you stay, forever young

She fell asleep on my lap . . . in my arms . . . as Billy made it through that door to safety.

Epilogue - 2010

I'd put Joanie to bed after "Forever Young" finished that night so many years ago, and stayed with her long enough to make sure she was still sleeping with her teddy bear gently snuggled alongside, resting on her arm.

And then . . . nearly twenty years went by in the blink of an eye.

⌣

It's near midnight and I'm sitting at my desk in a silent house with only the Pacific's rhythmic wave machine keeping me company. My novel is stuck in the same place it's been sidetracked for weeks now. It needs new ideas, a push onward. Wanting distraction, I slide my mouse over YouTube's side panel listing suggested next selections. There it is, "A Simple Twist of Fate." Dylan included it in his 1975, *Blood on the Tracks* album and Baez recorded it in the same year on her *Diamonds and Rust* album. With its superior instrumentation and arrangement, I like her version better; it rocks a little more. I click on it and am immediately mesmerized.

Taken literally, Dylan's story line in "Simple Twist of Fate" isn't my story, just as so many of his songs aren't my story either. But the song conjures up images for me that, taken in my context—probably out of his, whatever it was—have always been emotionally relevant for me. I never lost anyone because of some "simple twist of fate" as Dylan's words imply. But twists of fate had long ago brought first Sara, and then years later, Suze and Dianne to me. And then little Joanie.

Even if I never understood his meanings, and the Dylanologists shout that I've misused them, that's okay. I use them in a way that feels right because I've always been pretty sure that would be acceptable to him. It seems like a fair bargain: I love his music, but I want the freedom to interpret it in my own way. He certainly borrowed ideas and work from others; I think he would dig it. He has said the song wasn't about him or his failing marriage to his Sara. But he's said so many contradictory things about most of his music, who's to know? Maybe it's his gift to anyone who could use it in anyway it seemed to fit. That may be allowing a larger intent than is due, but why not? He had a touch for giving us things we all could use in our own ways, intended or not.

I don't believe he thought words he set to music reflecting his experiences and loves in Greenwich Village in the '60s would be fully understood by us out in the hinterlands then, or by those of later generations. Every artist wants his work to live beyond the places and times they were created. I've always taken that as freedom for others to use art as it fits their situations, different from his as they were then—or are now. So, forgive me if my uses seem off base, but I have taken that freedom.

Dylan never wanted to be pinned down by reporters, interviewers, friends, lovers—anyone. He never wanted to be defined, analyzed, characterized, or categorized. While he was doing that evasion thing of his with the rest of us, he kept his options open and all of us guessing. We're all still guessing today—even the Dylanologists.

I'm ready for it now. I want to let the music take me anywhere it will tonight. Yes, it used to take me to places that brought on melancholy and questions I had about myself and what I'd missed decades ago. But those weren't lost years—not in any sense. I loved Sara with all my heart. I still do. They were wonderful years that couldn't have been replaced with anyone, anywhere. And I love the three women who now call this weathered, jumble-block place on the beach home.

People tell me it's a sin
To know and feel too much within

I believe she was my twin, but I lost the ring
She was born in spring, but I was born too late
Blame it on a simple twist of fate

I admit that I've never figured out exactly why this song touches me so deeply, but it does. It made, and still makes, me feel—even if I can't identify why—something strongly. That's the important thing.

The End

Robert Gilberg

Acknowledgments

Other lyric segments used under Fair Use practice:

By Bob Dylan: One Too Many Mornings, p. 4; Queen Jane Approximately, p. 14; I Want You, p.28; You Ain't Goin Nowhere, p.31; To Ramona, p. 32; It's All Over Now Baby Blue, p. 35; It Takes a Lot to Laugh, It Takes a Train to Cry, p. 47; Like a Rolling Stone, p. 75; Knockin' On Heaven's Door, p. 99 and p.119; It's All Right Ma (I'm Only Bleeding), p. 111; I Believe in You, p. 140; If Not For You, p. 143; You Been on My Mind, p. 167; Forever Young, p. 209.

J Baez: Diamonds and Rust, p.1

K Reid: Whiter Shade of Pale, p 49

J Tempchin and R Strandlund: Already Gone, p. 171

R Orbison & J Melson: Blue Bayou, p.173

Cover image reprinted with permission of Fotosearch.

Inside title page image used with permission of Cara Schaefer.

Special thanks to my book doctor, friend, and sage: Anne Marie Welsh

This is a work of fiction. With the exception of the musicians mentioned in this novel, the names, characters, places, and incidents are all either the products of the author's imagination or are used fictitiously, and any resemblance to actual persons, living or dead, events, or locales is coincidental.

Robert Gilberg
San Diego, Ca.
June 26, 2017

Made in the USA
San Bernardino, CA
23 July 2017